FOX ON STAGE

by James Marshall

DIAL BOOKS FOR YOUNG READERS · NEW YORK

For Anita Lobel

Published by
Dial Books for Young Readers
A Division of Penguin Books USA Inc.
375 Hudson Street
New York, New York 10014

Copyright © 1993 by James Marshall
All rights reserved
Printed in Hong Kong by
South China Printing Company (1988) Limited

The Dial Easy-to-Read logo is a registered trademark of
Dial Books for Young Readers,
a division of Penguin Books USA Inc., ® TM 1,162,718.

Library of Congress Cataloging in Publication Data
Marshall, James, 1942– Fox on stage
by James Marshall.—1st ed.
p.   cm.
Summary: Fox makes a film for Grannie,
takes part in a magic show, and puts on a play.
ISBN 0-8037-1356-8.—ISBN 0-8037-1357-6 (lib.)
[1. Foxes—Fiction. 2. Performing arts—Fiction.]
I. Title.
PZ7.M35672Fq   1993   [E]—dc20   91-46740   CIP   AC

First Edition
1 3 5 7 9 10 8 6 4 2

The art for each picture consists of an ink, pencil,
and watercolor painting, which is scanner-separated
and reproduced in full color.

Reading Level 1.9

FOX ON FILM

When Grannie Fox had a bad spill
on the ski slopes,
she broke both legs.
"Grannie Fox will have to be
in the hospital for some time,"
said Doctor Ed.
"Old bones take longer to heal."
"Oh, what do *you* know?"
said Grannie.

But Doctor Ed was right.

Grannie had to stay in the hospital

for weeks and weeks.

"I'm so bored I could scream," she said.

"Grannie is down in the dumps," said Fox.
"We should do something to
pick up her spirits."
Then Fox got one of his great ideas.

"Louise and I are going to make
a video for Grannie," said Fox.

"How sweet," said Mom.

"But if anything happens to my camera..."

"I know what I'm doing," said Fox.

The next day the video was finished.

Fox's friends came for a look.

"This better be good," said Carmen.

"I'm very busy."

Fox put in the tape.

"Here I am taking out the trash,"
said Fox.

"This is me in my new shoes," said Fox.
"Hm," said Dexter.

"Me, flossing my teeth," said Fox.

"*How* exciting," said Carmen.

"Me again," said Fox.

"So we see," said Dexter.

"Care to watch it again?" said Fox.

"Certainly not," said Carmen.

"You've wasted our time."

"What was wrong with it?"
said Fox.

"It was *dumb*," said Dexter.

"I liked it, Fox," said Louise.

The next day Fox tried again.

He put a new tape in the camera

and set off.

This time he left Louise at home.

"You're so mean," said Louise.

Just down the block Fox filmed

Mrs. O'Hara trying on her new corset.

"Smile!" said Fox.

"Monster!" cried Mrs. O'Hara.

And Fox tore away.

Down a dark alley

Fox filmed some bad dogs.

They were up to no good.

"Catch that fox!" they cried.

And Fox tore away.

In the park Fox saw Officer Tom

smooching with his girlfriend.

"Nice shot!" said Fox.

"You'll be sorry!" cried Officer Tom.

But Fox got away.

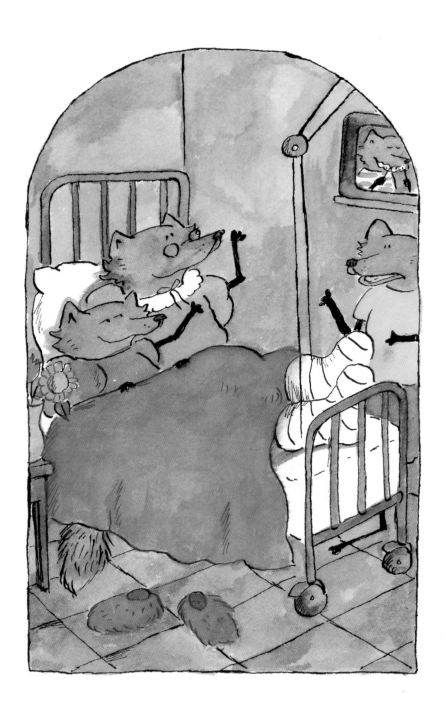

Fox went to the hospital

to show Grannie his new video.

But Grannie and Louise

were already watching one.

"This is Fox flossing his teeth,"

said Louise.

"Wow!" said Grannie.

"Don't watch that!" cried Fox.

"It's dumb!"

"What do you know?" said Grannie.

"We just *love* it."

At Fox's house some folks were waiting.

"That's him!" cried Mrs. O'Hara.

Maybe they don't like being
movie stars, thought Fox.
And he went inside to face the music.

FLYING
FOX

Fox and the gang

went to a magic show.

"I hope this guy is good,"

said Dexter.

"It's probably just a lot

of dumb tricks with scarves,"

said Fox.

"Anybody can do it."

And they sat down in

the very first row.

The lights went down.

And the curtain went up.

Mr. Yee, the World's Greatest Magician,
came forward.
"Welcome to the show,"
he said.
"Some parts will be *very* scary!"
"Oh, sure," whispered Fox.
"Let the magic begin!"
cried Mr. Yee.

First Mr. Yee did a trick with scarves.

"I told you," said Fox.

Then Mr. Yee made his helper vanish.

"Ho-hum," said Fox.

Next Mr. Yee pulled a rabbit from a hat.
"Big deal," said Fox.

Next Mr. Yee put his helper to sleep.
"This is *so* dumb," said Fox.

"What's all the chatter?" said Mr. Yee.

"It's Fox!" called out Dexter.

"You don't say," said Mr. Yee.

"Come up on stage, Fox."

"You're going to get it!" said Dexter.

Fox went up on stage.

"Sit here, Mr. Smarty," said Mr. Yee.

"Let's see how brave you are."

"Brave?" said Fox.

"Abracadabra!" said Mr. Yee.

Slowly the chair rose in the air.

"Where are the wires?" said Fox.

"No wires," said Mr. Yee.

"Only magic."

Fox held on tight.

And the chair flew all over.

"I'd like to come down," said Fox.

"Oh my," said Mr. Yee.

"I forgot how to do this part."

"Try Abracadabra!" said Fox.

"Abracadabra," said Mr. Yee.

Fox came gently down.

And the show was over.

At home Fox told Louise to sit down.

"Abracadabra!" said Fox.

The chair did not move.

"Rats!" said Fox.

"You just need practice," said Mom.

FOX
ON STAGE

One Saturday morning
Fox and his friends
were just lying around.
"What a sad little group,"
said Mom.
"Why don't you *do* something?"
"The television is broken,"
said Fox.
"Oh, that *is* terrible!"
said Mom.
Then Fox had one of his
great ideas.

"Let's put on a play!" he said.

"We can charge everyone a dime."

"We'll get rich!" said Dexter.

"I'll buy a new car," said Carmen.

And they went to the library.

"Let's do a spooky play," said Carmen.

"We can scare all the little kids."

"Here's what you need," said Miss Pencil.

"It's called *Spooky Plays*.

My favorite is 'The Mummy's Toe.'"

"Oooh," said the gang.

Fox and the gang went home to practice.

"The Mummy's Toe" was *very* scary.

Dexter played the mummy.

Carmen was the princess.

And Fox was the hero.

Soon things were moving right along.

Fox and Dexter worked hard
on the set.

And Carmen put up posters
all over town.

FOX
AND THE
GANG
PRESENT
"THE
MUMMY'S
TOE"

Mom and Louise helped out
with the costumes.
"Hold still," said Mom.
"I hope I'm scary enough," said Dexter.
It was time for the play.

Fox peeked out from behind the curtain.

There was a big crowd.

"I hope everything goes okay,"

said Dexter.

"What could go wrong?" said Fox.

The curtain went up.

And the play began.

Right away Carmen forgot her lines.

"Well I *did* know them,"

she said to the audience.

Then Dexter crashed through

the scenery.

"Whoops," said Dexter.

It was Fox's turn

to appear.

Suddenly it began to rain.

Fox's beautiful paper costume

fell apart in front of everyone.

"What do we do now?" said Carmen.

"Pull the curtain down!"

Fox called out to Louise.

And Louise pulled with all her might.

The curtain came down.

"Who turned out the lights?"

cried Carmen.

"Where am I?" said Dexter.

"The play is ruined!" cried Fox.

"*Everything* went wrong!"

The next day

Fox heard some folks talking.

"That Fox really knows how
to put on a funny show," someone said.
"Funniest thing I ever saw,"
said someone else.

And Fox began to plan his next show.

The Indian Americans

Other books in the
Immigrants in America series:

The Indian Americans

By Scott Ingram
and Christina M. Girod

LUCENT
BOOKS®

THOMSON
—✦—
                    ™
GALE

San Diego • Detroit • New York • San Francisco • Cleveland • New Haven, Conn. • Waterville, Maine • London • Munich

LIBRARY OF CONGRESS CATALOGING-IN-PUBLICATION DATA

Ingram, Scott.
    Indian Americans / by Scott Ingram and Christina M. Girod.
v. cm. — (Immigrants in America)
Includes bibliographical references (p.). and index.
Contents: Introduction: The importance of identity—The first wave—Indian immigration since 1965—The struggle to fit in—Maintaining an Indian identity—Between two
worlds—Forging a link with the American mainstream.
    ISBN 1-59018-270-7 (alk. paper)
    1. East Indian Americans—History—Juvenile literature. 2. East Indian Americans—
Social conditions—Juvenile literature. 3. Immigrants—United States—History—Juvenile
literature. 4. India—Emigration and immigration—History—Juvenile literature. 5.
United States—Emigration and immigration—History—Juvenile literature.
    (1. East Indian Americans. 2. Immigrants.) I. Title. II. Series.
    E184. E2G57 2005
    973'.0491411—dc21

                                                          2003001644

CONTENTS

Immigrants have come to America at different times, for different reasons, and from many different places. They leave their homelands to escape religious and political persecution, poverty, war, famine, and countless other hardships. The journey is rarely easy. Sometimes, it entails a long and hazardous ocean voyage. Other times, it follows a circuitous route through refugee camps and foreign countries. At the turn of the twentieth century, for instance, Italian peasants, fleeing poverty, boarded steamships bound for New York, Boston, and other eastern seaports. And during the 1970s and 1980s, Vietnamese men, women, and children, victims of a devastating war, began arriving at refugee camps in Arkansas, Pennsylvania, Florida, and California, en route to establishing new lives in the United States.

Whatever the circumstances surrounding their departure, the immigrants' journey is always made more difficult by the knowledge that they leave behind family, friends, and a familiar way of life. Despite this, immigrants continue to come to America because, for many, the United States represents something they could not find at home: freedom and opportunity for themselves and their children.

No matter what their reasons for emigrating, where they have come from, or when they left, once here, nearly all immigrants face considerable challenges in adapting and making the United States

their new home. Language barriers, unfamiliar surroundings, and sometimes hostile neighbors make it difficult for immigrants to assimilate into American society. Some Vietnamese, for instance, could not read or write in their native tongue when they arrived in the United States. This heightened their struggle to communicate with employers who demanded they be literate in English, a language vastly different from their own. Likewise, Irish immigrant school children in Boston faced classmates who teased and belittled their lilting accent. Immigrants from Russia often felt isolated, having settled in areas of the United States where they had no access to traditional Russian foods. Similarly, Italian families, used to certain wines and spices, rarely shopped or traveled outside of New York's Little Italy, a self-contained community cut off from the rest of the city.

Even when first-generation immigrants do successfully settle into life in the United States, their children, born in America, often have different values and are influenced more by their country of birth than their parents' traditions. Children want to be a part of the American culture and usually welcome American ideals, beliefs, and styles. As they become more Americanized—adopting Western dating habits and fashions, for instance— they tend to cast aside or even actively reject the traditions embraced by their parents. Assimilation, then, often becomes an ideological dispute that creates conflict among immigrants of every ethnicity. Whether Chinese, Italian, Russian, or Vietnamese, young people battle their elders for respect, individuality, and freedom, issues that often would not have come up in their homeland. And no matter how tightly the first generations hold onto their traditions, in the end, it is usually the young people who decide what to keep and what to discard.

The Immigrants in America series fully examines the immigrant experience. Each book in the series discusses why the immigrants left their homeland, what the journey to America was like, what they experienced when they arrived, and the challenges of assimilation. Each volume includes discussion of triumph and tragedy, contributions and influences, history and the future. Fully documented primary and secondary source quotations enliven the text. Sidebars highlight interesting events and personalities. Annotated bibliographies offer ideas for additional research. Each book in this dynamic series provides students with a wealth of information as well as launching points for further discussion.

INTRODUCTION

Across the Water

From the early colonial years to the dawn of the twenty-first century, much of American history has been shaped by immigrants. Other than Native Americans, the original inhabitants of the American continent, and African Americans, who were brought here against their will, all other Americans are either immigrants or the descendants of immigrants who have come to the shores of what is now the United States.

Of the groups that immigrated to the United States in the last half of the twentieth century, one has stood out for its rapid entry into mainstream American life. These are the Indian Americans, who have come to the United States in increasing numbers since immigration quotas were lifted in 1965. Since that time, educated and skilled Indian Americans have influenced many aspects of American life.

Growing and Successful

Today, the Indian American population has reached about 2 million people, slightly more than 0.8 percent of the U.S. population. The population grew rapidly between 1980 and 1990, but in the last decade of the twentieth century the number of immigrants from India more than doubled the group's population. According to the 2000 census, Indian immigration to the United States between 1990 and 2000 grew by more than 105 percent. This represents the fastest growth of any immigrant group from Asia since the first census was taken in 1790. In total numbers, Indian Americans are now the third largest Asian immigrant group in the United States, behind Chinese and Filipino Americans.

As the Indian American population has increased, Indian Americans have become one of the most successful immigrant

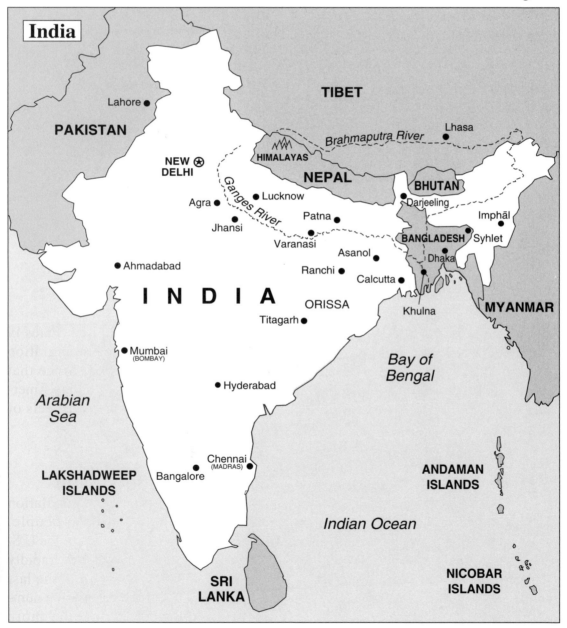

India

communities—economically, professionally, and socially—in U.S. history. In addition to holding the traditional jobs of immigrants as service workers or laborers, Indian Americans have filled the ranks of small business owners, high-tech engineers, managers of major corporations, physicians, scientists, hotel owners and managers, and technology entrepreneurs. Although they make up less than 1 percent of the U.S. population, Indian Americans make up more than 5 percent of all scientists, engineers, and software specialists in the country. No ethnic group has a higher per capita income than Indian Americans, and this success has largely been accomplished within a generation.

Although the history of Indian immigration to the United States is similar to that of other groups, there are key differences. One is that most Indian immigrants are fluent in English, because India is the third largest English-speaking country in the world. Another is their high level of education. Indian immigrants to the United States since 1965 are among the most educated of any immigrant group in history. About two-thirds of Indian Americans have completed college; almost half hold an M.A., Ph.D., or other professional degree.

Indian Americans like this father and daughter comprise one of the largest and most successful immigrant groups in the United States.

Challenges in a New Century

Despite the success of Indian Americans, life in a new land has proved difficult for many newcomers. Maintaining a balance between modern American life and Indian beliefs and lifestyles is a formidable challenge in a country where Indian religion, clothing, music, and other cultural traditions may be seen as strange and foreign.

The effort to benefit from life in America while remaining tied to tradition has been difficult for many first-generation Indian immigrants. In many cases, it has resulted in the social isolation of living only among their fellow Indians. Now, as the American-born second generation reaches adulthood, many Indian Americans wrestle with questions of identity, uncertain whether they are Indian, American, or a combination of both.

Asserting Their Position

Today, more and more Indians are merging into mainstream society. Gone are the restrictive immigration laws that kept Indians out of the United States for much of the twentieth century. Indian Americans are now widely acknowledged as one of the most vibrant and active immigrant communities in American society. From creating Hotmail, one of the largest e-mail service providers on the Internet, to winning the Nobel Prize for Economics, the success achieved by Indian Americans in a few decades is a testimony to their determination to achieve.

Yet despite their intellectual, financial, political, and social contributions, Indian Americans must continually reassert their position in society. This assertiveness has become especially critical in the aftermath of the terrorist attacks on the United States that occurred on September 11, 2001. Although no Indians were involved in the attacks, many Indians—especially Muslims—have been victims of prejudice and ignorance.

By their own achievements, Indian Americans stand as one of the most dynamic immigrant communities in American society, yet they struggle to gain acceptance as Americans. This tension has caused great concern among Indian Americans, who believe that they have earned the right to live among fellow Americans and be treated without suspicion. "[Indians] should not be driven into tight social enclaves," says social activist Debashish Mishra, chair of South Asian American Leaders of Tomorrow. "[We] must develop a voice that can shape public opinion. Since 9/11, we are on a cliff and hanging on to it by our fingers."[1]

CHAPTER ONE

From Mogul to Raj

The first recorded arrival of an Indian immigrant to the United States was a man from Madras who arrived in Salem, Massachusetts, in 1790 aboard a whaling ship. Between 1820 and 1898, about five hundred Indians immigrated to the United States. It may be surprising that, despite the minuscule Indian population that existed in the United States before the 1900s and the cultural differences between India and the United States, connections between the two countries go back to the early 1600s.

Colonial Connections

One major factor shared by the two countries is language. English became the main language in the United States and India because both were colonial possessions of Great Britain for many years. Although Indians continued to speak their native languages at home, most learned English in order to communicate with and serve their colonial rulers.

India came under control of Great Britain in the first decades of the seventeenth century. While English settlers were establishing tobacco plantations in Virginia, British traders sailed to India to establish trade in tea, spices, and textiles.

At the time the British arrived in India, the region was largely under the control of the Mogul Empire, one of the great civilizations in South Asia. The empire stretched from Afghanistan across what is today Pakistan and much of India. Although the Mogul rulers were Muslims, they allowed freedom of worship to followers of the Hindu religion who made up the majority of the Indian population. Politically, the Hindus were separated into several states that were ruled by Hindus but that paid taxes to the Mogul emperor—an arrangement that resembled the relationship between the colonies of North America and their British rulers in London.

In 1600, England's ruler, Queen Elizabeth I, had granted exclusive rights to the representatives of the British East India Company to trade with India. The East India Company's ships, however, did not arrive at the western port of Surat until 1608. The first British traders met with the Mogul emperor, Jahan-gir, who ruled from 1605 to 1627. Jahan-gir had inherited the throne from his father, but he was not a military conqueror like the earlier emperors. Instead, he spent much of his vast wealth to support arts such as painting, architecture, philosophy, and literature, which gained the empire its enduring fame. Indian, Muslim, and Western historians call this period the age of Mogul splendor.

While Jahan-gir was creating splendor, however, the British were creating a trading empire. By 1615, the emperor had granted

In the early seventeenth century, Emperor Jahan-gir (hunting lions, forefront) allowed the British to establish the East India Company at Surat.

the British permission to build a factory, or trading post, at Surat. The East India Company was thus able to take advantage of the highly developed Indian economy.

A Modern Empire

Unlike the first British settlers in North America, the British who went to India found a country that was in many ways more modern than European nations. According to historian Jacques Pirenne, "In the middle of the seventeenth century, Asia still had a far more important place in the world than Europe. . . . The riches of [India] were incomparably greater than those of the European states. Her industrial techniques showed a subtlety and a tradition that the European handicrafts did not possess . . . there was nothing in the [West] that [Indians] had to envy."[2]

In addition to taking advantage of the great skills of Indian cotton and silk weavers, the British East India merchants gained absolute control over the export of agricultural products such as sugar, indigo dye, and tea. The financial transactions of the company were greatly assisted by the services of wealthy Hindu and Mogul financiers. During the first half of the seventeenth century, the rule of Mogul emperors provided peace and security for the establishment of a healthy trading relationship.

Within a decade of building the factory at Surat, the company had established a trading outpost in the large city-state of Bombay. Located in northwestern India on a peninsula and islands on the Arabian Sea, it provided one of the best harbors on the western coast. By the mid–seventeenth century, the British company had established trade outposts and extensive trading routes in the coastal Hindu states of Calcutta and Madras.

Decline of Mogul Power

The British success in building trade relationships was partly aided by the growing tension between Hindus and the Mogul ruler Shah Jahan, who followed Jahan-gir to the throne in 1628. It was during the reign of Shah Jahan that the Taj Mahal was built—a burial chamber that is still considered one of the most beautiful buildings in the world. Unfortunately for the majority of Indians, Shah Jahan's desire to beautify his surroundings depleted his treasury. He was forced to impose a serious tax burden on Hindu farmers. (Muslims were not taxed according to religious custom.) During the final years of his rule, he raised the tax from 30 percent to 50 percent of the value of the crops grown on every piece of land. This move was deeply resented by the Hindus, who were largely poor farmers. This resentment, coupled with Shah Jahan's increasingly strict interpretation of Islamic law, played into the hands of the British traders, who offered Hindus employment and religious freedom in the areas they controlled.

The ruler who followed Shah Jahan to the throne also helped the British gather support from India's Hindu population. His name was Alamgir (known in the West by his princely title, Aurangzeb), and he, much more than his two predecessors, was a devout Muslim who did not believe in religious freedom. The new ruler punished Hindus who refused to convert to Islam and destroyed their temples and religious shrines. He also executed the religious leader of the Sikhs—a nationalist religion that had arisen in southeastern India.

In order to expand his control over much of India, Alamgir had to put down several revolts of Hindu ethnic groups across the country. The constant military campaigns continued to weaken the Mogul Empire after his death in 1707. As Mogul power declined, political disorder spread. Numerous

Sikhism

Sikhism is a religion that was developed in the northern Indian state of Punjab in the beginning of the sixteenth century. Its founder, Guru Nanak (*guru* is the Hindi word for "teacher"), combined the teachings of Hinduism and Islam to develop a faith based on the worship of a single god, a belief in the equality of all people, a prohibition of idol worship, and a respect for hard work. The early followers of Nanak founded the holy city of Amritsar in Punjab, where they constructed the first Gurdwara (literally "doorway to the guru"), the name by which all Sikh temples are known. The teachings of Nanak, along with the hymns of Hindu and Muslim saints and the writings of the other gurus, were compiled by early followers into the Guru Granth Sahib, the holy book of the Sikhs.

The relatively rapid formation and growth of the Sikh religion was met with alarm by the Mogul rulers in India. They perceived Sikhism both as a violation of Islam and a movement that threatened their hold on power. As a result, a number of early Sikh leaders were executed and Sikhism's existence was threatened. In the late seventeenth century, however, Sikh leader Gobind Singh gained a group of followers who were fiercely committed to defending the faith. These men became the first members of the Khalsa, or the Pure.

The Khalsa were given new names with the suffix *Singh*, or "lion," attached to each. As a mark of their devotion, they were required to wear the five symbols of Sikh faith: *kes* (uncut hair, which was kept under a turban), *kangha* (a comb), *kara* (a steel bangle), *kirpan* (a sword or knife), and *kachcha* (special breeches or undergarments).

Despite continued persecution under the Mogul emperor Alamgir (Aurangzeb), the Sikh community flourished, largely due to the fearsome reputation of its men as fighters. In the nineteenth century, the British enlisted the Sikhs to put down rebellions by other Indians who were sepoys. Eventually the Sikhs became the backbone of the British colonial army.

regional states arose, and much of the country was torn apart by war between local rulers who sought to create their own empires. In order to protect its interests, the East India Company recruited and armed its own private military force of Indian soldiers, called sepoys.

A Private Commercial Empire

During the era of colonization, it was not unusual for a country to hire private soldiers, called mercenaries. India, however, was unique in that its economy was now under the control of a private company with a private armed force.

The new, small, weak states were forced to pay the company's private force for military protection. Thus, the unusual alliance of small states and a colonial trading company became one of the most powerful political organizations in India. Eventually, the control of the East India Company extended inland from its coastal holdings into a number of small Indian states.

Meanwhile, the East India Company's main settlements in Bombay, Madras, and Calcutta had expanded from trading posts to commercial ports. Indian merchants and workers flocked to these areas to work for the company, interacting with the British who lived there. In the first decades of the eighteenth century, relations between Indians and British were extremely friendly. The East India Company had many employees from both countries, and strong social and business friendships arose. Marriage between British and Indians was not unusual. Many of the British employees of the East India Company adapted well to life in India. They dressed in Indian clothing, enjoyed Indian social activities, and absorbed local Hindi words into their own language.

During this same time, cotton cloth from the looms of Indian weavers was arriving in Great Britain in large quantities. The cheap, washable, lightweight fabric caused a revolution in clothing and furnishings. When British settlers in the colonies of the American South realized that their climate was perfect for growing Indian cotton, the plants were brought from India, and a pillar of the American economy of the South was established.

The economic growth in India as a result of cotton did not go unnoticed by the other European powers. As the profits of the East India Company increased over the first half of the eighteenth century, the French saw no reason why they should not share in the benefits of relations with India.

Conflict and Triumph

Efforts by France and other European powers to establish relations with India met with mixed success. Some independent states were economically and politically stable and were satisfied with the relations they had established with the East India Company. In some states near the coastal areas of India, however, rulers who wanted to expand their power turned to Europeans for support.

At that time, Great Britain's fiercest rival for world domination was France. For a number of years, ill will had existed between the two nations over claims in North America. That tension increased in the

Indian and French mercenaries fight Robert Clive's troops at Plassey for control of the large state of Bengal.

1740s, when opposing Indian rulers in southern India formed alliances with the British and the French.

Like the British, the French had formed a private company—the French East India Company. Like their British counterparts, French merchants established trade relations with various states in southern India and offered them the protection of a private armed force of Indians and French soldiers. Successful commanders of these private forces could earn enormous rewards for taking over reluctant states and placing an Indian ally on the thrones.

In the 1750s, the conflict between the French and British erupted into the French and Indian War in the American colonies. At the same time, private armies commanded by British and French mercenaries clashed in bloody battles in southern India. The key battle was fought by British troops under Robert Clive. In 1757, Clive defeated French mercenaries at the Battle of Plassey. This victory gave the East India Company control of the large state of Bengal.

The Rule of the Raj

The British victory at the Battle of Plassey began the period of rule in India known as the British Raj. This term, which means "king" in the Hindi language, signified that while the East India Company remained the primary economic force in control of India, the British government in London held overall power that resembled that of the Mogul emperors.

Not surprisingly, the enormous profits made by the East India Company had caught the attention of the British Parliament. Many in the government were uncomfortable with the notion of a private British company controlling an enormous country and reaping enormous profits while paying almost no taxes to the government treasury. Members of Parliament insisted that the leader of the legislature, the prime minister, should force the East India Company to submit its records and other information to the government for review. Some members of Parliament wanted the government to send an overseer to India to monitor the company's actions and to assure that all taxes owed to the government were paid.

Despite Parliament's concern about the activities of the East India Company, the British government was slow to act. The enormous distance between the two countries alone—it was a three-month ocean journey—prevented close oversight of the company. Meanwhile, across India, the managers of the company's trading settlements began to take on the role of provincial governors. Large sepoy armies were established in most provinces to crush any internal resistance.

The buildup of military forces in the provinces increased expenses for the company. This in turn forced them to look to the Indians for additional money—the same approach taken by Shah Jahan a century earlier. In many areas, peasant landowners were required to pay their taxes in cash rather than crops. This often meant that they had to borrow funds from moneylenders—both British and Indian. Inevitably, many peasants could not repay the loans and their land was taken for nonpayment. The number of landless peasants increased across India.

Logging by the British led to the further loss of land. Their purpose was to provide building materials for the rapidly growing trading centers as well as to drive Indians from the frontiers into cities, where they

Emperor Shah Alum receives Robert Clive. After the Battle of Plassey, Clive and the East India Company took control of India's economy.

could be more easily controlled. Those who did not go to the cities were forced to scratch out a meager existence on land that was increasingly eroded by rainfall that washed away topsoil unprotected by trees or other vegetation. Due to the loss of massive areas of farmland, the first large-scale famine struck the state of Punjab in the late 1760s.

The British Government Asserts Power

In the early 1770s, the British government again attempted to gain a share of the East India Company's profits for the British treasury. In 1773, Parliament passed the Regulating Act, which appointed a governor-general, also called a viceroy, to take charge of all company lands in India. This governor-general assured that profits were not skimmed before tax revenue was sent to London, a problem that had become apparent to many in the government. The first governor-general, Warren Hastings, immediately imposed governmental control over the company's activities.

The control was tightened in 1784, when the British government set up a control board for India. Under this arrangement, the East India Company controlled economic decisions, but the British government ruled India. In 1786, Hastings was replaced as viceroy by Lord Charles Cornwallis, the general whose surrender to George Washington had ended the American Revolution.

In India, Cornwallis increased the number of the sepoy troops and expanded the control of the company over provinces that had until that point escaped the British presence. Over the seven years he served as viceroy, Cornwallis crushed a number of rebellions against the empire, strengthening the British hold on India. He returned as viceroy in 1805 and died in India a short time later.

A New Century Dawns

By the time of Cornwallis's death, a number of British companies and citizens had begun to express strong objections to the exclusive control the East India Company had in India. Finally, after years of protest, Parliament voted to allow all British citizens and companies to open trading relations with India. Now, any British subjects who wished to immigrate to India did not have to be employees of the East India Company. Over the next thirty years, merchants, business entrepreneurs, and adventurers hoping to get rich immigrated to India in large numbers. Unlike the first British settlers in India, these new arrivals did not mix with the natives. The growing British population, however, encouraged by the viceroy, continued to acquire new lands to add to the colonial empire.

As large numbers of British subjects settled in India, the once-friendly relations between the two countries changed. Many in the British government believed that the British were naturally superior to the Indians. Thomas Macauley, a member of the control board, spoke for many British when he stated "that a single shelf of a good European library was worth the whole native literature of India . . . and . . . all the historical information . . . from all the books written in [India] is less valuable than what may be found in [textbooks] . . . used at preparatory schools in England."[3] British rule and education, government leaders such as Macauley claimed, would bring a system of law and a Western culture to a backward nation. It was during this period that all schools in India began to teach pupils in the English language. English also replaced Persian and Hindi as the language spoken by all public administrators.

As the British population in India grew and the racist attitudes among the new immigrants hardened, many Indian states were taken over by the British on the grounds that the Indian rulers were corrupt and unconcerned with the welfare of their subjects. Other territories, whose rulers died without a male heir, were also taken over by the British.

Although British rule was harsh and the conditions under which the majority of Indians lived were desperate, few Indians emigrated from the country during that time. One reason was a Hindu belief that forbade leaving India to cross the "black water"—the ocean. In addition, a British law passed in the early 1800s prohibited the movement of Indians from their native provinces. This was done to keep political activity localized, preventing any unified resistance to the British Raj.

Movements and Interest Abroad

Any emigration of Indians that did occur during the mid-1800s was controlled by the British—and was a result of British

---

Hindi or Hindu?

Many people who are unfamiliar with India confuse the terms *Hindu* and *Hindi*. Hindu is the largest religion of India, practiced by more than 80 percent of Indians. Hindi is one of the three main languages spoken by people in India—the others are English and Tamil. Hindi is related to the ancient Sanskrit language, which was spoken by the earliest inhabitants of northern India.

Hindi is written in a script called Devanagari, which means "the writing of the gods." The alphabet consists of twenty vowels, eight semivowels, twenty-five consonants, and sixteen compound consonants. Hindi sentences use a different word order than English. Verbs are placed at the end of a sentence, and postpositions are used rather than prepositions, meaning they come after the noun, as in these examples:

English: I learn Hindi. Hindi: Hindi I learn.

English: I go to the shop. Hindi: I shop to go.

Many English words are derived from Hindi, including *bandanna, bungalow, cot, curry, dungarees, khaki, pajamas, pundit,* and *thug.*

needs. For example, the first large Indian migration outside of the country resulted from Britain's need for plantation workers in the Western hemisphere and Africa. Following the abolition of slavery, Britain established a system of indentured labor. Under this system, Indians agreed to work for a set number of years in one of the British colonies of the Caribbean or Africa for low pay, lodging, and food. By the 1840s, large numbers of immigrants left India for Trinidad in the Caribbean; Guyana in South America; Mauritius, an island off the coast of Africa; and the South African colony of Natal.

These Indians agreed to leave their homeland largely because disastrous economic conditions had arisen in India during the mid-1800s. At that time, the East India Company still controlled a great deal of the huge nation. While British employees lived in relative comfort, the company had done little to improve or modernize the living conditions of Indians. In a speech before Parliament in 1858, John Bright, a social reformer and member of the House of Commons, compared a large English city with the areas of India controlled by the East India Company. "The single city of Manchester, in the supply of its inhabitants with the single article of water, has spent a larger sum of money than the East India Company has spent in the fourteen years from 1834 to 1848 in public works of every kind throughout the whole of its vast dominions."[4]

In agricultural areas under its control, the company was equally neglectful. Over the last half of the eighteenth century, as lands had come under its control, the company had built roads as well as canals to irrigate fields. Yet when the cost of maintaining those important public works cut into company profits, repairs were overlooked. In 1838, British author Gordon Thompson wrote that "roads and . . . canals constructed [by the company] for . . . the good of the country have [fallen] into dilapidation; and now the want of the means of irrigation causes famines."[5]

In fact, during the first half of the nineteenth century, more than 1.5 million Indians died of starvation in lands largely controlled by Great Britain and the East India Company. More and more people left the country because extreme poverty had spread across India.

Although few Indians settled outside of British-controlled lands, an interest in India started to develop in Western countries. This was especially true in the United States. Even though the Indian population in the United States was extremely small, American citizens became fascinated with Indian culture through travel books and newspaper articles.

Throughout the nineteenth century, plays that romanticized the relation between British rulers and Mogul kings, such as *The Rajah's Daughter* and *Cataract of the Ganges*, were among the most popular works performed in American theaters in the Northeast. Books on Indian culture and clothing fashion were best sellers. Famous American writers such as Ralph Waldo Emerson and Henry David Thoreau studied the Hindu religion. Poet Walt Whitman even wrote a poem titled "Passage to India," which compared that passage to the journey of his soul to a higher power.

The First Revolution

The movement of Indians and the growing interest in Indian culture, however, had little effect on the everyday lives of most Indians. The British hold on their nation was firm. Even among Indians who had avoided poverty and starvation, British rule had become unbearable. Most Indians were deeply conservative people who resented the British for insulting—or ignoring—Indian traditions and ways of life. Social reforms, Western laws, and, most offensive to these religious people, Christianity had been forced upon them. The longer the British ruled, the more determined Indians became to resist domination.

By the mid-1850s, resentment of British rule had spread to the sepoys. This anger eventually led to the bloody Sepoy Mutiny in 1857, the beginning of the long battle for independence. The revolt of the sepoys nearly overturned two centuries of British control. Over a few weeks in May 1857, territories along the Ganges River fell under rebel control. Both sides committed horrible atrocities, and Indian peasants as well as British civilians were victims of brutality.

Eventually, the power of the British army proved too formidable for the rebels. By mid-1858, the British had crushed the rebellion. Nevertheless, the violence marked a turning point for both sides. The revolt made the British realize that as long as they remained in India, they would face hostility. Most Indians realized that though

they had lost, the flame of independence and nationalism had been lit.

Another result of the war was the complete closure of the East India Company and its removal from any influence on policies regarding India. For the first time, India was governed directly by England, although the viceroy remained the figurehead in India. To win the approval of the Indians, Queen Victoria of England pledged that she and her representatives would work for the greater welfare of the Indian people. This assertion of British control from London began the final years of the Raj.

A Canal Brings England Closer

Many changes in Indian life during the latter years of the nineteenth century were a direct result of the opening of the Suez Canal in 1869. The hundred-mile waterway across Egypt connected the Mediterranean and Red Seas. This relatively short passage reduced the sea journey between England and India from three months to three weeks because ships no longer had to sail around Africa.

The shorter voyage brought more British women and children to India. By the 1870s, the British had developed a society in India that was totally separate from the native culture—and one that showed little respect for Indian traditions and values. For example, the sacred Taj Mahal was used by the British for balls, parties, and other frivolous activities. Although alcohol was forbidden by Muslim law, drunken British soldiers and civilians

South Asian Diaspora

In the middle decades of the nineteenth century, after the British abolished slavery, the need for laborers arose in areas that had once been worked by African slaves. In areas of the British Empire, the need for plantation workers was supplied by a system known as indentured labor. Under this system, Indians agreed to work for a set number of years—usually five—in a British colony. In return, the worker received a low wage, housing, and food. Most laborers who agreed to this arrangement came from areas of north-central and northeastern India that had been particularly hard hit by famine and disease. After their servitude ended, many indentured workers remained in the colonies to which they had been sent because there was more opportunity for work there than in India.

By the 1840s, laborers had arrived in Trinidad in the Caribbean, Guyana in South America, and Mauritius off the coast of Africa. By the 1860s, Indians were working farms in the British colony of Natal in South Africa. Eventually, groups of indentured workers were sent to Malaya and the Pacific colony of Fiji.

In 1920, the British Parliament abolished the indentured worker system. By that time, millions of Indians lived in areas scattered across the globe. This era of mass exodus from India is known to Indians as the South Asian Diaspora.

were a common sight on the grounds of the shrine. It was not unusual for British visitors to chip off pieces of the beautiful structure for mementos.

The opening of the Suez Canal also caused economic problems for India. A shorter passage meant that ships could bring more British goods to India. To make certain that the goods sold, they were assessed import duties of 4 percent, while Indian goods exported to England were assessed duties of up to 70 percent. When citizens of both countries began to buy goods from Great Britain rather than India, the resulting trade imbalance changed the entire structure of the Indian economy. Millions of spinners, weavers, potters, and other artisans lost their livelihood. An entire class of Indians saw centuries-old traditions gradually disappear. By the end of the nineteenth century, approximately 90 percent of the Indian population was composed of landless agricultural workers.

The increasing desperation of many Indians gave added support to the movement for Indian independence that had begun in 1857. In 1885, members of the independence movement formed the Indian National Congress. This association of Indian government officials, lawyers,

The Sepoy Rebellion

Although revolts against the British occurred sporadically during the nineteenth century, the Sepoy Rebellion in 1857 was the bloodiest and most widespread. The basic causes were economic unrest and British disrespect for Indian culture. The final push toward violence was instigated by the use of animal grease on the ammunition cartridges in the newly issued Enfield rifles used by the Indian troops. To load these rifles, soldiers had to bite off the end of the cartridges. The sepoys heard that the cartridges were greased with beef fat and pork lard. Since the cow is sacred to Hindus, and the pig is considered unclean by Muslims, the sepoys were outraged.

Early in 1857, three regiments were disbanded and eighty-five sepoys were imprisoned for disobeying orders to load their rifles. This led to a mutiny by several regiments in May 1857. Although the mutiny began spontaneously, it became more organized and spread quickly. By June, nearly ninety thousand Indian soldiers, or 70 percent of the British sepoy force, had rebelled. The sepoys took over the cities of Delhi and Kanpur.

During the early stages of the revolt, the British regular troops were caught by surprise and suffered heavy casualties. After major losses at the Kanpur garrison and Lucknow, the British army,

The Sepoy Rebellion was the bloodiest Indian revolt against British rule.

along with remaining largely Sikh sepoys, regrouped. Eventually, the rebellion was harshly crushed by the British. On September 20, 1857, the British recaptured Delhi and, in the following months, their forts at Kanpur and Lucknow. The British victories were accompanied by widespread revenge. Many unarmed sepoys were bayoneted, sewn up in the carcasses of pigs or cows, or fired from cannons.

and other professionals from the small, English-educated middle class was established to provide Indians with a voice in the government.

Many Indians, however, did not want a voice in a government controlled by the British. They wanted the British to leave India. The desire for independence attracted radicals who supported the nationalist cause but did not believe in peaceful political change. In the final years of the nineteenth century, while economic conditions deteriorated throughout the country, several states were torn by campaigns of terror and assassination that targeted British officials as well as civilians.

CHAPTER TWO

The First Wave

The unrest and poverty that had spread across India by the late nineteenth century drove the first substantial numbers of Indians to emigrate from the country. At the same time in the United States—long a destination of the world's immigrants—a railroad network linking the Pacific Northwest with the rest of the country was being built. Laborers were needed to complete the difficult work. As a result, the states of Washington and Oregon, as well as areas of western Canada, became the destination for the first wave of Indian immigrants. This flow of emigrants from India peaked around 1904 and continued at a steady pace until 1914, when the U.S. government closed the nation's doors to Indian immigration altogether.

Fading Colonialism in India

In addition to the lure of work in America, many Indians left their homeland because of dismal conditions there. By the late 1890s and early 1900s, British colonial policies had resulted in the deaths of millions of Indians from starvation and disease. By 1910, the average life expectancy of an Indian had fallen to twenty-five years.

The disaster stemmed largely from a particular British colonial policy employed throughout the 1800s—the export of grain to supply England. In the late 1800s, the British Empire steadily began to lose control of colonies that had met Great Britain's needs for grain and other agricultural products. As a result, the government turned to India, the largest of its remaining colonies, to make up the crop shortfall. In the last three decades of the nineteenth century, the export of wheat, rice, and other agricultural products from India increased by 400 percent. Much of the land in the northern states of Punjab and Bengal that had produced grain for the population there was placed under the control of British landlords, who sent the grain to Great Britain.

With a huge amount of food being exported, the people of India faced almost continuous famine. In the second half of the nineteenth century, India suffered twenty-four famines. Between 1876 and 1900 alone, eighteen famines resulted in the deaths of more than 20 million people, according to official British records. In a book titled *Prosperous British India*, written in 1901, author William Digby wrote that "famines and scarcities have been four times as numerous, during the last thirty years of the 19th century as they were one hundred years ago, and four times as widespread."[6]

Unrest Spreads

With millions of people dying and most unable to leave the country, the Indian independence movement became stronger. Small groups of educated Indians began to advocate outright independence. British officials tried to suppress such inflammatory talk by arresting those who spoke out in its support. Instead of quelling the talk of independence, however, measures of this sort forced the Indian nationalist movement underground. Moreover, the movement decided on other means of action when its members realized that their protests would not be readily heard. Few anti-British radicals believed that the powerful British army could be defeated. Thus, the nationalist leaders turned to the one area that they knew would harm British interests—the economy.

Over the final decades of the nineteenth century, British manufacturers had made huge profits from the sale of their goods in India. Many Indians who supported nationalism decided that a boycott of (a refusal to buy) imported British goods would harm the British economy in the country. To manage the boycott—called *swadeshi* in Hindi—a group called Pritam Dharma Sabah was formed. In the early 1900s Sabah members helped to set up worker-run shops that processed sugar and made items such as soap and cloth, which had previously been imported from Great Britain.

In August 1905, a nationwide boycott of foreign goods was proclaimed. The boycott was accompanied by other protests against the British rule. Indian merchants refused service to English patrons—cobblers refused to mend their shoes, and washers would not clean their clothes.

By late 1905, anti-British leaders in the states of Bengal and Maharashtra not only insisted on the boycott of British goods, they also called on Indians to refuse to pay all colonial taxes. To emphasize their determination to force out

Nineteenth-Century Famines

In the final three decades of the nineteenth century, much of India suffered through a prolonged period of drought that weather experts now believe was caused by a change in the flow of the El Niño ocean current. As a result of the drought, the monsoon rains upon which India's farmers depended did not occur as usual. Between 1876 and 1891, drought struck huge agricultural areas of India four times.

Famines had occurred before in India's history, but they were usually localized, and, although thousands of people died, the overall impact was not widespread in the enormous country. In addition, both the Mogul rulers and the early owners of the British East India Company offered food and other assistance to areas hard hit.

One of the most influential British officials during the famines was the notorius Lord George Curzon. He held office first as secretary of state, then as secretary for foreign affairs, and later as viceroy of India. While in power, Curzon introduced a series of reforms that upset his civil servants. He not only refused to offer assistance to famine-struck regions, he insisted on raising the prices for food that was available there in order to increase the crown's revenues. It is estimated that the combination of widespread drought and colonial policies resulted in the deaths of 15 million Indians in the final years of the nineteenth century.

Between 1876 and 1891, millions of Indians starved to death as a result of drought, famine, and cruel colonial policies.

the British, workers went on strike, and women joined students to protest in front of any stores that sold British goods. Over time, growing numbers of Indians of all religions and social classes attended meetings of anti-British groups and took part in street processions.

Because the anti-British protests were widespread and relatively effective, British viceroy Lord George Curzon resorted to a scheme he called "divide and rule" to blunt the protests. In 1905, Curzon divided the state of Bengal into two separate states. East Bengal's capital was Dacca, while West Bengal's capital at Calcutta also served as the capital of British India. The partition outraged Bengalis. Because East Bengal was Muslim and West Bengal was Hindu, Curzon not only divided the states, he created a separation of religion. He further separated the people by bribing undercover agitators to initiate bloody riots between Hindus and Muslims. The religious conflicts added to the misery of the Indian people.

Punjab Disorder

As disconcerting as the Bengal protests were to the British, the spread of the discontent to Punjab, a desert plains region in the north, made the British even more uneasy. There the boycott and refusal to pay taxes became especially heated. This was a particular concern because for much of the British rule, Punjabi men had been the backbone of the British army, at times constituting half of the sepoy troops. The Punjabis were also skilled farmers, and the British counted on Punjab's farms to grow

enough crops to feed the army and to export to Great Britain.

When the Punjab region was devastated by famine, anti-British protests there became especially angry. In May 1907, crowds led by students and striking workers in the Punjabi city of Rawalpindi marched through the streets. The Indians threw mud and stones at British civilians and Christian missionaries and attacked government offices, British company offices, and commercial buildings. The uprising was stopped cold by well-armed British troops who fired into the crowds. Colonial police and troops ruthlessly crushed uprisings in the cities of Lahore and Amritsar. Arrests and prosecution of Indian patriots followed, and a state of emergency was declared in a number of Punjab districts.

Making the Decision

As conditions worsened in Punjab, many Punjabis left India for better opportunities elsewhere. They heard that in America and Canada a worker could earn from $2 to $2.50 a day, a vast fortune compared to their meager income of 10 cents a day in India. Lured by promises of lumber and factory jobs on the west coast of North America, streams of Indian peasants migrated to the United States and Canada. As these immigrants settled into their new life, they sent reports of their incomes and lifestyles back to their families in India. These accounts often exaggerated the immigrants' success in order to persuade family members to immigrate too.

As a result of these reports and as unrest spread across Punjab, even more Punjabi

In the early twentieth century, British soldiers like these met with fierce resistance in India's Punjab region. Poor living conditions there drove many Indians to rebel against the British.

peasants immigrated to North America during the first decade of the twentieth century. More than half of these immigrants arrived in California and worked as farm laborers. Others went farther north to Oregon and Washington to work on railroad construction. After that work was completed, many found jobs in timber mills and steel factories.

The decision to immigrate was not an individual decision. Because the cost of the passage had to be raised from relatives' contributions and loans, all members of the family participated in the decision. Often, the family member who immigrated was a young man who left his wife and children behind under the care of the extended family, because the cost of passage for an

entire family was far more than many Indian families could afford. The price ranged between three hundred and four hundred rupees, about seven dollars—more than three months' pay for a one-way trip. After arriving in America, few men had their wives or children join them because of the uncertain living conditions and the arduous work.

A Difficult Journey

After securing the money and bidding farewell to family, the immigrants set out by train east to Delhi, where they boarded another train southeast to Calcutta. The men usually went by steamship from Calcutta to Hong Kong, China, a journey of twelve days. After a wait that sometimes lasted a month, they boarded a passenger ship bound for Vancouver, Canada. The sail across the Pacific Ocean from Hong Kong to Canada or the United States lasted another eighteen or nineteen days.

The ocean journey was extremely difficult for many immigrants. Most of them stayed in steerage, the compartment set aside for the lowest-paying passengers. This section was usually crowded, damp, and unsanitary. The food prepared on the ship was European, and many immigrants would not or could not eat it, either because they did not eat meat for religious reasons or because they could not digest the food, which made them ill.

Eventually, immigration restrictions were put in place in Canada, which sent more immigrants directly to California.

There they passed through the Angel Island station in San Francisco Bay. Although Americans at the time considered this island an immigration checkpoint similar to Ellis Island in New York Harbor, (the entry point for millions of white European immigrants), conditions were actually much more primitive. In fact, Angel Island resembled a prison camp. A number of strict anti-Chinese immigration laws had been passed in the late 1800s, and people of Asian descent who arrived on the West Coast were held in confinement until they could prove they were not Chinese citizens. While Indian immigrants waited at the processing point, they were crowded into filthy barracks with little food or water. In 1910, Luther Steward, acting commissioner for the Immigration

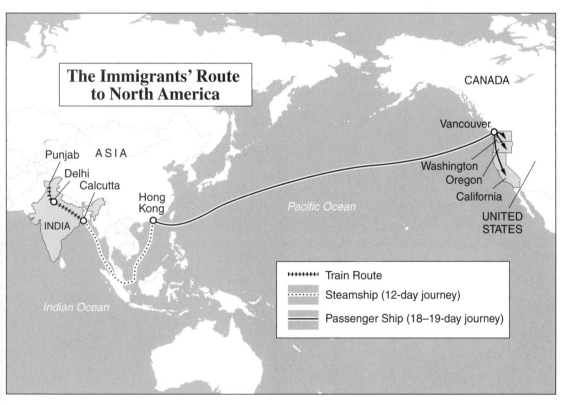

The Immigrants' Route to North America

CANADA

Vancouver

Washington
Oregon
California

UNITED
STATES

Punjab   ASIA
  Delhi
  Calcutta
              Hong
              Kong
INDIA

Pacific Ocean

Indian Ocean

┣┼┼┼┼┼┤ Train Route
·············· Steamship (12-day journey)
━━━━━ Passenger Ship (18–19-day journey)

Service in San Francisco, wrote of the barracks: "If a private individual had such an establishment, he would be arrested by local health authorities."[7]

Life in a Foreign Land

Whether they landed in Canada or California, immigrants immediately searched for work. Many who landed in Canada found the climate too cold compared to India and crossed the border to Washington. There they earned from $1.35 to $2.00 a day working in lumber mills, laying railroad lines, or clearing land for the railroad. The few who spoke English—most immigrants were poor farmers from Punjab who had not been educated in the British system—were sometimes fortunate enough to obtain work as a foreman for $2.50 to $3.00 a day, which was more than they could earn in two weeks in India.

No matter what work the Punjabi men first took, they were eventually drawn to the farming areas of California. California offered an irresistible opportunity to men who had grown up as farmers. Since many came from families that owned or leased land, the possibility of obtaining land was a driving force in their lives. The enormous central valleys of California offered an almost limitless supply of land and work to eager immigrants.

What made the California landscape even more attractive was its resemblance to Punjab, which relieved the immigrants' homesickness. One immigrant, Puna Singh, wrote this impression of California: "On arriving in the Sacramento Valley, one could not help but be reminded of

Many Indian immigrants were drawn to agricultural jobs in California's fertile valleys and fields. Here, immigrants take a break from picking grapes in a California vineyard.

the Punjab. Fertile fields stretched across the flat valley to the foothills lying far in the distance. Most of the jobs available were agricultural and I found many Punjabis already working throughout the area."[8]

By the end of the first decade of the twentieth century, Punjabi immigrants were migrating around California in work groups. Each group appointed a leader who spoke English to obtain work for them. Like migrant workers everywhere, they followed the harvests throughout the year, beginning in the Sacramento Valley, where they worked in orchards, vineyards, and sugar beet fields. From there they traveled south to the vineyards and citrus groves of the San Joaquin Valley in central California. Finally they ended up in the Imperial Valley of southern California, working in the cantaloupe and cotton fields.

Mixed Reception

Although the new immigrants appreciated the higher wages they could earn in their new homeland, many soon faced a challenge: prejudice from white Americans. The prejudice took many forms, from simple ignorance to biased government policies to violence. Most whites, for example, referred to the Indian immigrants as "Hindus" or "Hindoos" although 85 percent of all immigrants were followers of the Sikh religion.

The open racism of the time was expressed by many. Most active in the anti-immigrant movement were the members of the Asian Exclusion League (AEL), who considered Indians and other Asian immigrants a threat to white Americans.

The league, originally formed to combat immigration by Japanese and Chinese people, pressured their local, state, and national lawmakers to limit Indian immigration.

The AEL succeeded in getting a law passed that limited the number of female Indian immigrants admitted to the country. Allowing married men to bring wives and daughters, said AEL leaders, would lead Indians to settle permanently in America. As a result of this legislation, in the first decade of the twentieth century, only twelve Indian immigrants were women.

The AEL further objected to Indian immigrants working in the United States because they sent much of the money they earned back to their families in India, unlike white workers, who kept their money in the American economy. The AEL also accused the immigrants of taking jobs from whites by working for less money in worse conditions.

All of these factors aroused resentment, fear, or, at the very least, curiosity among white Americans. An article from the *Daily Astorian*, a local paper in Astoria, Oregon, recorded the thoughts of longtime residents who remembered the arrival of the Indian immigrants, who lived in an area known to Americans as "Hindu Alley." The residents' comments reveal the mixed reception the immigrants received:

Mention the Hindus to an old-timer, and the immediate response is, "Yes, remember them. They all wore white turbans. . . ." Many of the old-timers reported that as children, they were afraid of the Hindus. "We thought

American Interest in India

Although based more on myth than reality, interest in India spread across the United States during the late nineteenth-century. Much of the interest centered on Indian religions, including Buddhism, which had begun in India but was practiced mainly by other Asians.

As a result of this curiosity about Indian culture, the Indian religious leader Swami Vivekananda attended the World's Parliament of Religions in 1893 in Chicago. A powerful speaker who dressed in the flowing orange robes of a Hindu sannyasi (monk), he became a celebrity. American citizens, largely ignorant of the terrible famine and other disasters in India, responded strongly to his demand that Great Britain grant independence to India.

As newspaper stories spread about the swami's speeches on the welfare of Indians, reporters were sent to India to provide firsthand accounts of the situation there. American charities sent aid to India during the famine of 1897. The Americans' respect for Swami Vivekananda encouraged many Indians to leave India and pursue their spiritual quest in the United States. Hindu ashrams—places of retreat—such as the Ramakrishna Vedanta Centers were established in the late 1890s in Chicago, Rochester, Cleveland, Pittsburgh, Detroit, and other cities.

they were terrible coming with their turbans," said Mrs. [Hattie] Spencer. "We were afraid of them at first. But my dad said, 'They have to make a living as the rest of us. We are foreigners, too.'"[9]

Although there were occasionally peaceful relations between whites and immigrants, they were overshadowed by a powerful anti-immigrant attitude among both citizens and lawmakers. Under pressure from the AEL, for example, the Oregon legislature passed a law in 1907 stating that Indians could never become permanent residents of the state. Virtually everywhere along the Pacific Coast, Indian immigration, which the AEL and others included under their racist term for Asians, "the yellow peril," was perceived as a threat to the white population. A newspaper editorial stated, "on the far out-posts of the Western world rises the specter of the yellow peril. . . . It is nothing more or less than a threatening inundation [flood] of Hindus over the Pacific Ocean."[10]

Competition and Discrimination

By 1907, the reception of Indian immigrants had taken a decidedly negative turn. That year hundreds of Indians came to America to escape a plague that killed half a million people in Punjab. Worried about the arrival of Punjabis, many Americans wanted to end Indian immigration.

The concern of many American workers was that what had at first seemed a very limited source of competition was now showing signs of becoming a threat as the number of immigrants increased. If large numbers of Indians settled in the United States, the efforts of American workers to achieve wage increases might fail. A strike would be ineffective, they contended, if immigrant replacement workers were available.

It was more than just a willingness to work for less, however, that attracted employers to Indian immigrants. Many employers considered Indian workers more dependable and harder working than American workers. Whereas many American workers stayed just long enough to get some experience and then moved on, Indian workers remained longer because their job choices were limited. Furthermore, Indian workers who needed to take time off would arrange for someone to replace them on the job.

Indians met a great deal of hostility from whites, especially those who resented their solid reputation as workers. During the Indian influx of 1907, the AEL organized parades of white workers to march in opposition to the Indian workforce. One bitter lumber mill worker vowed, "One of these days, by God, the whites are going to chase all of them out of camp and they won't come back either. We'll drive them all down the line with a two-by-four."[11]

Indian immigrants reacted to the growing hostility in different ways. Some Sikh men broke their religious vows by discarding the turbans they had worn since their baptism, cutting their hair, and wearing Western-style garments. They hoped to pass for Hispanic or Portuguese, since members of those groups, in spite of their dark skin, were considered "white." However, most Sikhs refused to give up their Sikh identity. As a consequence, Sikhs continued to be subjected to hostility and outright harassment from white workers.

The Anti-Hindu Riot and Its Effects

Whites' resentment of Indian immigrants eventually exploded on September 4, 1907, in a mob attack that became known as the Anti-Hindu Riot. That afternoon, mill workers in the port city of Bellingham, Washington, circulated a flyer urging white residents to drive the immigrants out of town. That evening, between four hundred and five hundred white men gathered to attack the Bellingham neighborhood where Indians lived. Many Indians were beaten. Some fled from their quarters in their nightclothes and sought shelter on the chilly beach. Others were forced out of the city limits or even jailed. More than seven hundred Indians fled the United States for Canada. Throughout the violence, speakers spurred the crowd to drive out the so-called cheap labor.

Unfortunately for Indian immigrants, the Bellingham riot was not isolated. Instead, it reflected a growing animosity toward Indian workers. In the months following the incident in Washington, for example, assaults against Indians occurred in Marysville, Stege, Live Oak, and other

California communities where immigrants had settled. The destruction caused by rioters stirred fear in factory owners and large-scale farm owners that their property would be at risk if further riots occurred. As a result, many immigrants who were considered good workers lost their jobs because employers feared potential violence.

Faced with competition from white factory workers, many Indians turned to agricultural work. In rural areas, especially in California, there were few white farmworkers. Indians could live in small, isolated communities relatively free from harassment and from the influence of the AEL.

There, many Indians were able to establish themselves as dependable farm laborers and frugal money managers. To save money, immigrants lived together in dormitory-like bunkhouses where one person was hired as a cook. They invested their money wisely, rarely going into debt for luxuries. In areas where they remained for any length of time, Indians established business relationships with bankers and lawyers. Thus they were able to obtain loans and use the legal system to file property deeds, verify contracts, and carry on similar activities.

Indians found that rural California suited them. Many prospered. By 1920, Indian immigrants in California owned, 2,099 acres of farmland and leased 86,340 acres. Most of the land was in the Imperial and Sacramento Valleys, where Indians grew fruits and vegetables as well as cash crops like cotton and rice.

By 1920, the arrival of the first wave of Indian immigrants had ended. Although

Land Ownership and Evading the Alien Laws

The Punjabis who settled in the Imperial Valley of southern California were adept at finding ways to get around the state's alien land laws that made land ownership by Indians illegal. The Punjabis studied the American legal system for loopholes and formed business alliances with American citizens who helped them get around the law. The primary strategy was to have the American citizen purchase the land on paper, but then hand it over to the Punjabi immigrant, who retained control of the land's operation and profits in reality if not in name.

The Punjabis successfully built their land ownership networks until 1933, when a grand jury indicted sixty-five Indians for conspiracy to evade the law. However, in 1934 the Supreme Court ruled that the state of California could not use that law in land ownership cases, thus making it impossible for any other Punjabis to be indicted. From then on, until citizenship was granted in 1946, the Imperial Valley Punjabis continued to "own" their own land.

most of the immigrants, eventually settled in the western United States, especially in sparsely populated areas of California, the perception of them as a threat to the state's economy remained. In a report by the California Board of Control, an immigration panel, Indians were referred to as "a group of laborers becoming landowners and threatening the monopoly of the majority group."[12] Unfortunately, this view would prevail during the coming decades.

CHAPTER THREE

Decades of Uncertainty

Hostility over jobs was often directed at Indian immigrants, but actually few whites lost work to Indian immigrants. In fact, few Indians immigrated to the United States in the early twentieth century; between 1899 and 1913, only seven thousand men emigrated from India to the United States.

Although the number of Indian immigrants was much less than the number of immigrants from Europe at the time, Indians and other Asians were treated with prejudice at all levels of American society. Even national figures such as President Theodore Roosevelt, Secretary of War William H. Taft, and Senator Henry

Cabot Lodge approved of the raids on Indian living areas.

Setbacks and Gains

These men, like many other Americans, claimed that the Indians were responsible for economic difficulties facing American laborers at the time. As anti-immigrant groups aimed their anger at Indians, immigration declined rapidly in the second decade of the twentieth century. From a high of 1,701 immigrants in 1908, the number of Indians who came to America fell to 172 in 1914. Thus began a long period in which

The Indian Caste System

One main difference between India and America—and a factor that appealed to many Indian immigrants—is the lack of caste systems in the United States. Castes are social ranks that are determined at birth by one's family lineage. Although there are thousands of castes in India, there are basically four levels of rank, ranging from high to middle to low to very low, each associated with certain types of occupations. People in the very low ranks are referred to as "scheduled caste" members, and they make up about 16 percent of the Indian population.

Each caste has its own dharma, or divinely ordained code of conduct. Generally, the higher the caste, the higher the expectations for proper behavior. Transgressions of the conduct code are dealt with by temporarily or permanently labeling the person as an outcast. If someone marries below his or her caste, that person's rank is lowered to that of the spouse.

People of higher ranks receive more privileges than those of lower ranks. Caste is most easily observed at a wedding feast, at which all residents of a village are usually present. All guests are seated in rows, with members of equal castes sitting together. Members of low castes, such as leather workers, are seated far from higher caste members and may even end up in an alley. The lowest-ranked caste members, such as launderers, usually have to wait for the other diners to throw their leftovers in a basket outside.

Although the Indian government has made discrimination on the basis of caste illegal, unequal treatment between caste ranks continues to exist in everyday life. Although the law now allows low caste members to read and to enter Hindu temples, those of higher castes still often treat them like second-class citizens.

Indians both in India and the United States faced uncertainty.

While the number of Indians in the United States dwindled by 1913, the Indian American population achieved a significant victory that year in a Supreme Court case, *United States v. A. Kumar*. In that case the Supreme Court decided that Indians were technically Caucasian, that is, white-skinned, rather than Asian. This ruling allowed a number of Indians to become naturalized citizens.

On the other hand, much legislation at the time worked against Indian immigrants. Under the California Alien Land Law of 1913, only citizens had the ability to buy, sell, or lease land, and most immigrants had not yet become citizens. Many immigrants who owned or leased land in California were required to give it up.

Many Punjabi farmers responded to the law by marrying Mexican American women who held citizenship. These marriages helped Indians gain acceptance because Mexicans were the largest minority in the state, and California had a long tradition of Hispanic culture from its years as a Spanish possession. Marriage to a citizen exempted Indians from the land law. Nevertheless, this merger of Indian and Hispanic backgrounds slowly eroded the Indian culture from areas of California in which it had been a visible presence.

Trouble in India

With the start of World War I in 1914, few people in India were willing to leave home during such tumultuous times, especially to go to the United States, which was clearly prejudiced against them. Even the number of immigrants who lived in America diminished as they chose to leave the hostile country. This, however, did not mean that conditions had improved in India.

As the remaining Indian Americans struggled to make a new life in America, their families faced similar and more deadly struggles in India. At the outbreak of World War I, many Indians volunteered to serve in the British armed forces. India provided more than a million soldiers and laborers to serve in Europe, Africa, and the Middle East. Indian princes contributed large supplies of food, money, and ammunition.

The awesome brutality of the war, however, quickly ended Indian support. High casualty rates, economic depression caused by heavy taxation, a worldwide influenza epidemic, and the disruption of trade during the war made the terrible suffering in India many times worse. The disastrous situation revived both moderate and extreme independence movements in India.

Faced again with Indian protest, the British cracked down hard. In early 1919, Parliament passed the Rowlatt Acts, called the Black Acts by Indians, which gave the viceroy the power to censor the press, hold political activists without trial, and arrest individuals without a warrant. The passage of the acts resulted in a nationwide strike of workers led by Mohandas K. Gandhi, a lawyer raised in South Africa and educated in Great Britain who was among the earliest leaders of the Indian nationalist movement.

The *hartal*, as the nationwide strike was called, signaled the widespread popular discontent. The bitter feelings between the British rulers and Indian subjects led to violence on April 13, 1919, in the city of Amritsar, Punjab. There, an unarmed crowd of some ten thousand men, women, and children had gathered to celebrate a Hindu festival. Most in the crowd were unaware of the prohibition against public assemblies under the Rowlatt Acts. Nevertheless, the British commander ordered his soldiers to open fire at point-blank range. Nearly four hundred Indians were killed and more than eleven hundred wounded in what came to be called the Amritsar Massacre.

The events of 1919 resulted in increased anti-British activity by Indians as well as stern antiprotest measures by British authorities. In 1920 Gandhi was sentenced to four years in jail for his role in the strike, and by 1921 an estimated three thousand Indians were in prison for treason. Ultimately, however, the drastic measures of the British colonial leaders did not crush the independence movement.

The Ghadar Movement

The independence movement had strong support among the Indian American community. In fact, much of the force for change came from the Indian American community, which was largely Punjabis.

In 1913, as immigration restrictions closed the doors of the United States to Indians, immigrants in San Francisco founded an Indian nationalist group called the Pacific Coast Hindustani Association. This group of farmers, students, and workers became known as the Ghadar Movement (*ghadar* means "revolt" in Hindi). Their goal was the liberation of India from British rule and the establishment of a democratic government.

The group published a newspaper called the *Ghadar* that printed articles on living conditions in India as well as racial issues

Supporters of Mohandas Gandhi demonstrate against British rule. Most Indian Americans supported the independence movement in India.

in the United States. To draw support from the Indian immigrant community, the group also circulated pamphlets and posters. These explained the Indians' grievances against the British:

> Our commerce and industry has been ruined. They [the British] have plundered and looted . . . and brought famine and plague. . . . these British strangle us in India. And when we come abroad here they also make our lives miserable. . . . Now the British are pressuring the American government to stop us from coming to the shores of America. . . . Brave Hindis [sic]! Awaken from your sleep. The British are getting you thrown out from everywhere. Let us unite and fight so such laws are not passed here [in the United States].[13]

The Ghadar Movement was unusual for a number of reasons. It was the first Indian political organization to call for total independence from British rule—and yet it originated in the United States, in large measure because its founders greatly admired the philosophy expressed in the Declaration of Independence. Although most of its members were Sikhs from Punjab, the movement expressed no regional or religious favoritism, unlike previous movements. Sikhs, Muslims, and Hindus were welcomed without bias.

Initially, the Ghadar drew great support from the immigrant community and was widely admired in India. Then, in 1915, movement leaders arranged a loan from the German government that was used to finance an arms shipment to India. The weapons were intended to be used in a planned uprising against the British. The arrangement was discovered by American authorities, however, and members of the Ghadar were charged with organizing a military expedition against a U.S. ally.

Fallout from the Ghadar Trial

In the trial that followed, fifteen Indian Americans were found guilty and sentenced to prison terms. Worse for the party was that it had drawn the attention of the American press and public. Politicians, responding to the news of the Ghadar plot, began to support exclusion laws for Indian immigration.

Pressured by the Asian Exclusion League (AEL), local and state politicians passed a series of laws that discriminated against immigrants and discouraged their efforts to become residents. On the national level, the Immigration Act of 1917 barred Indian immigrants from entering the United States. This law blocked new immigrants from countries listed in the designated "barred zone," one of which was India. The only exception to the law was that family members of Indians already living in the United States could be eligible to immigrate. However, in 1924, the passage of a new immigration act refused admission even to those family members.

Perhaps most demoralizing of all was the ruling in the *United States v. Bhagat Singh Thind* case in 1923. This Supreme Court decision stated that Indian immigrants were ineligible for citizenship.

The *Komagata Maru*

Workers and politicians in the United States were not the only people who wished to put a halt to Indian immigration in the early twentieth century. Canadians in the western province of British Columbia also fought immigration. The Canadian government responded to this resentment against Indian immigrants by passing extremely strict immigration laws. After 1907 emigration from India virtually stopped. While more than twenty-six hundred Indians entered Canada in 1907, only six were admitted in 1908.

Indians felt that they had a right to enter Canada. They claimed that as British subjects they should be allowed to immigrate to any country in the British Empire, which included Canada at that time. To test the Canadian law, a wealthy Punjabi business owner named Gurdit Singh arranged for a Japanese ship, the *Komagata Maru*, to take 376 British subjects—24 Muslims, 12 Hindus, and 340 Sikhs—to Vancouver.

When the *Komagata Maru* arrived in Vancouver on May 23, 1914, it was denied entry. The ship remained docked in the harbor for three months. Meanwhile, Indians in Canada and the United States collected contributions of money, food, and other aid for the ship's passengers while lawyers argued the case in Canadian courts. Eventually, the exclusionists won the case, and the government ordered the ship to leave Canadian waters.

When the ship landed at the port station of Budge Budge at the mouth of the Hooghly River, back in Calcutta, British officials assumed that the passengers would be angry with Gurdit Singh for leading them on the unsuccessful voyage. Instead, the voyagers had become even more loyal to Gurdit Singh and were enraged at their treatment at the hands of the British government. When authorities tried to force the passengers onto trains to continue the trip home, a violent confrontation broke out in which more than twenty men, both Indian and British, were killed. Many of those who had made the voyage were imprisoned, including Gurdit Singh. Today, a memorial to the voyagers of the *Komagata Maru* stands in Calcutta.

Singh, who had immigrated to the United States from northern India in 1913, had worked his way through the University of California at Berkeley and then fought in the U.S. Army during World War I. Returning from the war with an honorable discharge, Thind applied for citizenship in 1919. His application was initially approved by the U.S. District Court, based on the fact that Thind was technically Caucasian, or white. Because northern Indians are light-skinned and considered white, they were eligible for citizenship. At that time, citizenship was granted to people who were labeled white, brown, or black.

However, the Bureau of Naturalization appealed to the U.S. Supreme Court. It decided that although Indians are clearly Caucasian, they are from the Asian continent, which in the racial categorization of the day made them "yellow." The presiding judge decided that because Indians were not white, the legal basis for excluding them from citizenship existed because they were not from any of the other backgrounds necessary for citizenship. In a unanimous decision, the Supreme Court, using the term *Hindu* to refer to all Indians, declared, "It is a matter of familiar observation and knowledge that the physical group characteristics of the Hindus render them readily distinguishable from the various groups of persons in this country commonly recognized as white."[14]

The *Thind* decision had a devastating effect on Indian immigrants who had already been granted citizenship. Based on the new interpretation of the law, the federal government revoked the citizenship of several thousand Indian Americans. In addition, under the California Alien Land Law, some immigrant landowners whose citizenship had been revoked were stripped of their property. Some landowners, however, managed to keep their property by holding it or leasing it under the names of American lawyers, bankers, or farmers whom they trusted.

As a consequence of anti-immigrant laws, Indian immigration essentially came to a halt for almost two decades. By 1940, there were slightly less than twenty-five hundred Indian Americans living in the United States. During those years, some Indians continued to enter the country illegally by crossing the border from Mexico. Smuggling networks helped immigrants get across the border for a fee. Smugglers usually asked immigrants to shave their beards and remove their turbans to keep their ethnic background inconspicuous.

The Door Slowly Reopens

During the two decades in which there was almost no Indian immigration, many Americans underwent a change of attitude regarding independence for India. That change, in turn, affected their attitudes toward Indian immigration. In the 1920s, Americans generally supported British rule in India. The nonviolent protests of Gandhi and his followers, however, won wide support. At the same time, organizations across the United States, such as the Home Rule League and the India Association, campaigned vigorously for Indian independence and for citizenship for Indian Americans. The Ghadar Party rebuilt its reputation and pressed for the independence of India through peaceful means.

Successful immigrants also built support for the Indian cause. Mubarak Ali Khan, a wealthy Arizona farmer, made numerous appearances before Congress to argue that India should be independent from Great Britain, comparing the Indian struggle to that of the American colonists in the American Revolution. Sardar Jagjit Singh, a successful New York business owner, arranged for Senator Claire Booth Luce to travel to India. He also convinced her to use the pages of the magazine she owned, *Time*, to print articles supporting Indian independence.

These combined efforts eventually yielded success. By the late 1930s immigration sentiment had begun to change again. The key change in attitude came with the outbreak of World War II. When the United States entered the war in late 1941, the need for Asian allies to battle Japan prompted the U.S. government to foster good relations with India.

To gain the support of India, Congress suggested that the country become a dominion, which meant that it would be a self-governing nation with British ties, like Canada and Australia. Strong opposition from Britain, the Americans' primary ally, made it necessary to back down. Still hoping to gain access to Japan through India, the United States deployed troops to India in 1943 and 1944 with British permission. Seeking permission from Great Britain rather than India for this move, however, convinced many Indians that America agreed with British imperial policy. Disillusion with the United States grew among the Indian population, and by the end of the war in 1945, Indians were rioting against American troops stationed there.

The anti-American riots signaled that India was boiling over with resentment about its status as a colony. Many in the U.S. government feared that a war between India and Great Britain on the heels of World War II might draw Americans into the fighting. This fear persuaded U.S. lawmakers of the need to show Indians goodwill by allowing them to immigrate to the United States. Thus, American politicians tried to push through a number of bills to reverse the immigration exclusion laws.

Finally, in 1946, the U.S. Congress passed the Luce-Celler Act, which eliminated the total ban on Indian immigration and allowed Indians to become naturalized citizens. Although the act resulted in an average of only one hundred to two hundred Indian immigrants per year, now the wives, children, and other relations of Indians already in the United States could join them. Some of the older immigrants who had remained bachelors traveled back to India to marry and returned with their new wives.

First Steps to Second Wave

While there was a slight improvement in immigration law in the late 1940s, an enormous change took place in India itself. In 1947, the British realized that freedom for India was long overdue. On June 3, 1947, Viscount Louis Mountbatten, the governor-general, announced that the British Indian Empire would be divided into the nations of Hindu-dominated India and Muslim-dominated Pakistan. On August 15, 1947, India officially became an independent nation.

With India's independence from Great Britain, the relationship between India and the United States changed. New legislation created an opening for greater Indian immigration. By 1948, new federal laws allowed aliens in the United States the right to own land.

Even after India became the largest democracy in the world on January 26,

A convoy of American troops rolls along an Indian road near the Burmese border during World War II. Many Indians resented the American presence in their country during the war.

1950, when it approved a constitution, many Indians left their new nation to immigrate to the United States in search of opportunities in a more stable environment. This choice was made easier by the U.S. Immigration and Nationality Act of 1952, which encouraged the immigration of people with engineering, scientific, or medical skills. Gradually, Indians began to enter American society, and because these immigrants often had professional careers, they established themselves in middle-class neighborhoods. Thus began the second wave of Indian immigration, which brought almost sixty-five hundred Indians to the United States between 1948 and 1965. This wave almost tripled the Indian American population.

The increase in the immigrant population encouraged Indians to acknowledge their ethnicity, rather than seeking to disappear into other minority populations. Indian tradition flourished in immigrant communities: women wore native clothing, immigrants spoke native languages at home, and attendance at Sikh and Hindu temples rose. Indian immigrants felt special pride in 1956 when Dalip Singh Sauad, born in India, became the first Asian elected to the U.S. Congress.

Once the door to America had opened, a new interest in Indian culture arose in the United States. Americans became interested in the history, religions, and arts of the subcontinent, and when India's first prime minister, Jawaharlal Nehru, visited the United States, he spoke to crowds across the country.

India Faces Problems

Nehru's nation faced serious challenges in the 1950s. The division of colonial India into India and Pakistan led the two nations to battle over boundaries, water resources, and control of the northern

Final Steps to Freedom

The course of the final wrenching steps to independence for India was first set in 1913 by Indian immigrants who founded the Ghadar, the first political organization to call for complete independence from Great Britain. A year later, in India, the Muslim League was established by Indians who called for a separate state for the nation's Muslim population. From that point until eventual independence, not only was India torn by violent political protests, but its independence movement was bitterly divided between the Indian National Congress, which supported the Ghadar principles, and the Muslim League.

By the beginning of World War II, the struggle against British rule had led to strikes, peasant uprisings, and massacres. In 1942, the Indian National Congress issued the Quit India declaration, demanding that Great Britain grant independence to the nation. The Quit India Movement drew support across the country from people of all classes and religions. The anti-British sentiment became more unified than ever before.

After World War II ended in 1945, more than twenty thousand members of the Indian navy deserted their posts and went on strike in the nation's three largest cities. In Bombay, more that two hundred thousand factory workers joined the naval strike. By late 1946, the British were prepared to allow India its independence, and the final step was taken in 1947.

province of Kashmir. The subsequent war cost millions of lives. Additionally, Muslim and Hindu refugees abandoned a huge amount of property as they fled to either Pakistan or India.

Within the new borders of India, Nehru's government faced great difficulties merging the separate states into a cohesive nation. When the British left India, more than 560 independent states formed the country. Fewer than 20 became part of Pakistan. Thus, India became an enormous nation of competing kingdoms, languages, and cultures.

For India's leaders, economic development was as challenging as national unity. After centuries of colonial exploitation, India was at an economic disadvantage, with little manufacturing capability and a growing population trapped in poverty. Simply feeding India's people—the population surpassed the 1 billion mark in 2000—was an almost impossible task, and although India has been producing increasing amounts of food since the 1950s, the nation has yet to become economically self-sufficient.

Nehru's death in 1964 came before he had been in office long enough to address the many problems of a young democracy. Within a year, his daughter, Indira Gandhi, took office as India's prime minister. She immediately faced Muslim uprisings in the northeast, as well as famine, labor unrest, unrelieved poverty, and a separatist movement in Punjab. As a result, she was forced to implement strict policies that stifled political dissent and made her very unpopular.

During the administration of Nehru, about sixty-five hundred Indians had come to the United States. In the early stages of Gandhi's rule, the United States further eased immigration laws that had been in place for years. Few Americans anticipated that this change, coupled with the events in India, would contribute to a growing wave of Indian immigrants who arrived on American shores.

CHAPTER FOUR

The Second Wave Grows

In the mid-1960s, the U.S. Congress eased restrictions on immigration from many nations, including India. The new laws made it easier not only for people to join relatives already in the United States, but also for those seeking professional advancement to gain entry. Large numbers of Indians set out for the United States.

The new immigration law gave priority to family reunification, attracting those with needed skills, and refugees, in that order. Those who were not close relatives of citizens could now enter the United States if they could fill jobs in certain professional fields where there was a shortage of qualified American workers. As a result, the majority of the new Indian immigrants were college-educated and prepared to work in fields such as engineering, medicine, and scientific research.

Why They Left India

By the 1960s, India was still struggling to become a modern nation and to care for the majority of its citizens. Living conditions had improved since the first years of independence, and the development of industry and technology had been substantial. However, India still suffered from political unrest, exploding population, poverty, and religious conflict.

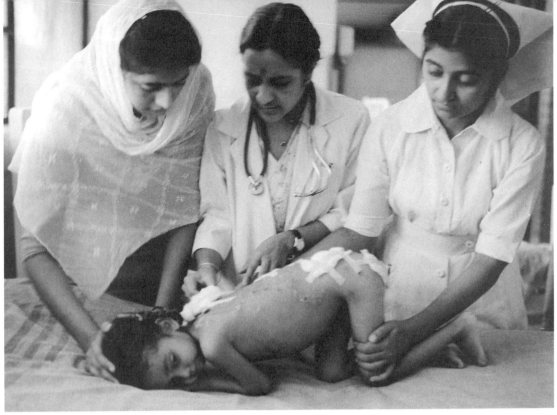

An Indian doctor treats a child injured in a Pakistani air strike. During the mid-1960s, wars, crop failures, and a struggling economy prompted many to leave India.

During the 1950s and early 1960s, most of India's engineers and scientists had been able to find steady employment. By 1965, however, the effects of the population boom, crop failures, and the heavy expenses of wars with Pakistan and China overwhelmed the Indian economy. Meanwhile, the American economy was relatively healthy, which caused the demand for professionals, particularly in engineering and medicine, to outstrip the supply.

As India's economy soured, some of its most talented professionals faced the prospect of unemployment as companies downsized or went bankrupt. They joined the throng that left to try their luck in a new land. For many Indians, the decision to immigrate was a matter of survival. As incomes diminished, were lost, or simply failed to keep up with inflation, many Indians found it difficult to pay for housing, clothing, food, and other daily necessities. Even Indian professionals whose jobs were secure found few opportunities for advancement in India. This led some people to become so dissatisfied with their jobs that they were willing to leave their homeland.

Education in the United States

Some Indians left, not with the idea of relocating permanently, but with a plan to attend college in the United States and then return to their native land. For many of these young people, the experience of arriving in a foreign country differed from, and was more pleasant than, that of other Indian immigrants. One advantage the students had, of course, was that they knew exactly where to go when they arrived in the United States, which often made the experience less traumatic and confusing.

More importantly, these students were welcomed by other students and were made to feel comfortable in college communities, in much the same way as high school exchange students from foreign countries are welcomed during their brief stays in the United States. Many Indian students appreciated the friendly reception they received from young Americans.

In the mid-1960s and early 1970s, it was common for Indian students to be met by a student welcoming committee as soon as they got off the airplane. They were then whisked off to the college campus, where they were allowed time to adjust to dormitory life—a challenge for all new college students. Ramesh, an Indian American, had this typical experience. Arriving as a student, he was greeted at the airport by people from his new university. They took him to the campus, helped him get settled, and told him where he could meet other Indian students. He immediately felt welcome in his new home, but also appreciated the opportunity to seek the company of students who shared his Indian culture.

Some students were fortunate enough to be welcomed by extended family or Indians from their home region already living in the United States. In this way, they had the support of other Indians as well as the acceptance of other young people who were also beginning college and were thus sharing the same experience.

Alka, an Indian American who came to the United States in the 1960s, had such an experience. She first lived with relatives' friends in the United States and was immediately impressed by the high standard of living that was possible in America. When she moved into a college dormitory, she felt comfortable because, although there were cultural differences, the other girls accepted her and made it easy for Alka to talk to them. The most difficult part of adjusting to American college life, Alka says, was adhering to the Indian tradition of strict separation of the sexes in public. Her solution was "to relate with boys but . . . refuse to go out [on dates] with boys."[15]

Some students encountered culture shock in their day-to-day life. One student, Amit, was shocked when his dormitory roommates changed their clothes in front of each other—something that violates Indian custom. He was so uncomfortable with occasionally seeing his roommates' nakedness that he ended up moving out of the dormitory and into the apartment of an Indian friend. Nevertheless, Amit's feelings of isolation continued for months after his arrival: "Everything was so different. . . . I missed my home, my people in India. . . . I used to cry at night and had trouble sleeping for quite some time."[16]

Whether or not these young people had good initial experiences in the United States, many Indian students became reluctant to give up the high standard of living after graduating from college. Many decided to seek entry-level jobs in America. They found themselves tempted to stay

Reflections on Immigration

Although the experience of immigrants arriving in the United States varies with each individual, most immigrants agree that the transition to a new country alters their lives in enormous ways. The following is an excerpt from poet Meena Alexander's book The Shock of Arrival, *in which she describes the changes she experienced upon entering the United States at the age of eighteen:*

The shock of arrival is multifold—what was borne in the mind is jarred, tossed into new shapes, an exciting exfoliation of sense. What we were in that other life, is shattered open. But the worlds we now inhabit still speak of the need for invention, of ancestors, of faith. In a time of literally explosive possibilities, we must figure out how to live our lives.

The shock of arrival forces us to new knowledge. What the immigrant must work with is what she must invent in order to live. Race, ethnicity, the fluid truths of gender are all cast afresh. Nationality, too, that emptiest and yet most contested of signs, marks us.

The old question "Who am I?" returns—I am what others see me as, but I am also my longings, my desire, my speech. But how is that speech formed, when what they see me as cuts against the grain of what I sense myself to be?

in the United States permanently, unwilling to give up their job security, professional satisfaction, and a standard of living to which they had become accustomed.

Making the Decision

Although college students did not necessarily know whether they would remain in the United States, many other Indians made a decision to reside permanently there. Just like those who immigrated in the early twentieth century, Indians leaving home in the 1960s did so after deep reflection and consideration of many important issues. The primary difference in the second wave of immigration was that this immigration was not just men. Entire families were faced with the decision of leaving their homeland.

Married couples with children, for example, worried about how American culture would affect their children. Husbands were concerned that their wives would leave behind not only their homeland, but the traditional roles established for them in Indian society. Adult men and women worried about being separated from members of their extended family, which went against the customary close ties that existed among Indians.

Those ties, while not unique to Indians, are one of the most enduring of all cultural traditions in India. The belief that close contact with relatives should be cultivated is shared by most Indian families. Indian children, for example, expect their parents to be involved in their lives, to aid in decision making, to assist with college tuition and living expenses, to arrange marriage partners, and to help with new babies. The very notion of "relative" is far-reaching, encompassing not only blood relatives, but friends from the same town or village. Thus, leaving India meant, in a manner of speaking, shutting off a support system.

Although most Indians spoke English, they shared little else culturally with Americans. Religious differences between Hindus from India and Christians, who were the religious majority in America, were vast. Observant Hindus practiced vegetarianism, for example, while that diet was not widely practiced in the United States in the 1960s. Thus, the decision to leave India, even for a high-paying job or a possibility of professional advancement, was not easily made.

Arrival Experiences

The experiences Indian immigrants had on arrival in the United States varied considerably, depending on whether they had lined up a job or living situation ahead of time. Some had a job and even a home waiting for them when they got off the plane; others struggled for a time to get settled. For many job seekers, figuring out where to settle down was not so simple. Although they were directed to cities in which many jobs were available, they were not offered any guidance on how to seek specific professional jobs. Thus some immigrants found themselves working

temporary jobs while they looked for something better. An Indian immigrant recalled his experience: "When I came here, I was prepared to do anything. I knew I had to be flexible. I did not get any engineering job, let alone professional job in the first year. I did odd jobs but never thought of going back."[17]

Regardless of what sort of job an immigrant found in the United States, the first year was often difficult, fraught with the pain of separation from loved ones and feelings of isolation in an unfamiliar culture. That sense of isolation was often particularly acute for those individuals who had left their spouses and children in India while they searched for a suitable job or place to live.

The spouses—mostly wives—who did immigrate expressed mixed feelings about their new life in the United States. For many, the excitement and opportunity of a new life in a wealthy country enabled them to make the momentous decision to leave. On the other hand, many quickly became homesick for their loved ones in India and complained of having no close friends with whom they could talk openly about their problems and worries. They, like their husbands, often felt like outsiders in American society. As a result, they felt shy and reserved around Americans. A number worried that their skills in English were inadequate and therefore avoided talking or spending time with neighbors. One woman explained, "We stand out. We wear saris [traditional Indian women's clothing]. We look different. . . . I experience a sense of 'I don't belong here.' I don't feel involved here. Sometimes I feel homesick."[18]

That sense of isolation tended to linger, especially among adult immigrants. They were apprehensive about being accepted in American society and continued to perceive themselves as outsiders. As one immigrant said, "Very few Americans accept you as their own in the first generation. . . . Apart from the professional meetings, there is very little social acceptance. . . . Some time, some families might accept you, but there is some barrier somewhere. There are some basic differences."[19]

Where They Settled

Unlike the first wave of Indian immigrants who settled in widely separated rural regions of the West, many Indians in the second wave were attracted to cities. Metropolitan areas of the United States were home to large companies that were hiring immigrants trained in scientific and technical fields. New York City, Los Angeles, and Chicago quickly developed large, thriving communities of Indians.

Not all immigrants opted for settling among their fellow Indians. Smaller suburban and rural communities attracted immigrants who were willing to take work wherever it could be found. For example, Indians trained as physicians often moved to towns whose doctor had retired or moved away, or to towns that had never had a local doctor.

Regardless of where they settled, Indian immigrants worked hard to carve a niche for themselves in their new communities. Especially in cities where large numbers of Indian immigrants settled, they sought each other out and began to develop distinct "Little India" neighborhoods with shops that sold foods and imported goods from India, Hindu, and Sikh places of worship, and other reminders of their homeland. These eased their struggles to fit into American society.

The Elderly Immigrant

Many elderly Indian parents followed their children, who sponsored their immigration, out of India in order to spend their retirement years close to family. As a result, between 1986 and 1993 about 20 percent of Indian immigrants were over fifty years of age. In Padma Rangaswamy's book Namasté America, *one elderly immigrant described his reasons for coming to the United States:*

We always wanted to be with our children in our last days—whether they are in Bombay or Delhi or here [in the United States]. The children wanted to come here. . . . Even in India, we would have liked to live with them. Because in your old age, there are many problems, with which no one other than your children can help you whether they are good or bad. But if the children don't desire it, we don't want to live with them. They should also want it, to give us love and respect. If not, we would prefer to live in India.

During the 1960s, many Indians settled in large cities like New York, Los Angeles, and Chicago. These immigrants established close-knit communities like Chicago's Indian district (pictured).

The English Advantage

The second wave of Indian immigrants, which increased enormously after 1965, had an easier time adapting to the American way of life than other ethnic groups traditionally have had. One attribute gave them an advantage over other minorities. Most could speak English fluently, since India's government had long encouraged people to study English as a means of easing communication in a country where eighteen different Indian languages were spoken. Thus, most Indians learned to speak English as children.

Having a command of the English language helped Indian immigrants assimilate in the United States in a variety of ways. It made the Indian immigrant more comfortable than other immigrants who could not speak English when they arrived in the United States, which is often a confusing and frightening experience.

Being able to speak English also gave Indian immigrants the power to communicate effectively in the pursuit of jobs—from filling out applications in English to completing successful job interviews with English-speaking company executives. It contributed to their success on the job by enabling them to communicate with colleagues and clients. It also eased the stress of adjusting to daily life in their new community, from buying what they needed at the grocery store to asking for street directions.

Finally, being able to speak and read English made it easier for Indian immigrants to participate more fully in American society. Being literate in English meant that they could read magazines and local newspapers, educating themselves on events in the nation and their community. Likewise, they could watch television and participate in social events.

Besides being able to speak English, many of the immigrants were well-educated and often found work in high-paying fields. However, despite these relative advantages to ease their entry into American life, Indian immigrants encountered cultural differences that sometimes created conflict at work, at school, and in social situations.

One source of conflict for Indian immigrants was the tendency of white Americans to be inconsistent in their expectations about the new arrivals. On one hand, most Americans valued the image presented by highly educated, professional Indian immigrants. Some sociologists and other observers, as a result, referred to Indians as a model minority. On the other hand, many whites saw the darker skin and different cultural traditions of Indians as setting them apart from whites and other races. Being considered a model minority has often meant that Indian immigrants were not wholly accepted by any social group—neither the white majority nor the various other minorities.

Historian Padma Rangaswamy explains the conflict that arises from the model minority designation:

[Indian Americans] are only too keenly aware that the label divides them along class lines (not all Indians are high-achievers), sets them against other minorities (so whites can ask

"Why can't blacks and Hispanics achieve like Asians?"), and deprives them of the resources they feel they are entitled to (they get cut out of affirmative action programs because they supposedly don't need them). For the majority of the non-Asian population, Indians may be an ethnic group distinct from Chinese, Koreans, or Japanese, but the ability of Indians to buy homes and operate businesses in their neighborhoods is increasingly dependent on public perceptions that are influenced by such stereotyping of Asian Americans.[20]

Assimilation Issues

Although Indians were familiar with Western culture, many still faced a difficult adjustment to American society. The emphasis in American society on the importance of individual and personal success directly conflicted with essential Indian values. These values were more complex—less oriented to the individual and more toward the group, which included extended family and members of the community. In *India: A Country Study*, author James Heitzman writes that Indians

are born into groups—families, clans, subcastes, castes [social classes], and religious communities—and live with a constant sense of being part of and inseparable from these groups. A corollary is the notion that everything a person does properly involves interaction with other people. A person's greatest dread, perhaps, is the possibility of being left alone, without social support, to face the necessary challenges of life.[21]

The contradictions that resulted from the desire to assimilate and the desire to remain true to Indian roots often created obstacles for immigrants. Indian immigrants who began a successful career in the United States were forced to decide how much independence they were willing to assert while still meeting the needs of their family and community.

For many, this meant being aggressive at work, but stepping back into traditional roles outside of work. Both men and women had certain roles that were expected of them at home within the traditions of Indian culture. Men generally took care of business and financial matters for the family. They generally set the rules about discipline and education for their children, budgeting the family income, and other matters that were often joint decisions when made by other American couples. A woman was expected to cook meals for her husband and children and to submit to her husband's decisions regarding family matters.

As Indian Americans became more settled in America, the contrast between being American and being Indian was most obvious to young children who had not absorbed much of the traditional culture or learned the standard gender roles before coming to America. One young immigrant, Anar, remembered that her mother, coming home from work, was expected to make tea for Anar's uncle and grandparents, who lived with them after Anar's father died. Anar's mother pressured her to also make tea: "I remember [that] they'd always get me to learn how to be a good . . . girl. Whatever that was. Like it was

The Measure of Success

In a February 2000 presentation, Rafiq Dossani, a consulting professor at the Stanford University Asia/Pacific Research Center, cited several measures of the economic success achieved by Indian immigrants in the United States.

In terms of financial success, the median family income for Indian Americans is $60,093. This is more than 50 percent higher than the national median of $38,885.

In education, at least 58 percent of Indian Americans over the age of twenty-five hold a bachelor's degree or higher. Over five thousand university faculty members in the United States are Indian Americans.

The high level of education has translated into success in the workplace. Over 43 percent of employed Indian Americans work in managerial or professional jobs. Another 33 percent work in technical, sales, and administrative support occupations.

really important that I made tea for them. . . . I'd come home from school, and this was a big thing. I was supposed to make tea for them. I was annoyed."[22]

For other immigrants, assimilating meant improving their standard of living to match that of other Americans. Many dedicated themselves to their work, not for personal glory, but as a way to achieve a better life for their family. Many Indian immigrants viewed the time and effort spent at work not as a sacrifice, but as a simple necessity for the family's sake. As one male immigrant explained, "I have to keep late hours, put in extra hours. Most of the time I have to work on weekends. . . . But I feel that I don't have any choice. . . . My professional success is going to help my family—more money, more comfort."[23]

Immigrants were attracted to America by the almost mythical possibility that one could succeed through hard work, regardless of class. For many Indian immigrants, this attraction was especially appealing because they had left a nation with strongly delineated social classes that did not offer such opportunities. In the United States, it seemed, anyone with ambition could achieve.

CHAPTER FIVE

Evolving Indian Values

In some ways, the experience of Indian immigrants has paralleled that of other immigrant groups as they have struggled to adapt to a new culture that is ignorant of their traditions. To resist the transformation of their culture, they turned to fellow immigrants as a link to the life they left behind. Immigrants formed organizations to reinforce traditions and advocate for the rights accorded to all people.

Building a Community Infrastructure

Without extended families nearby, and confused about conflicting cultures,

many Indian immigrants who came to the United States after 1965 turned to their fellow Indians for support. Organizations such as the Pacific Coast Khalsa Diwan Society and the Indian American Forum were founded to provide for the emotional and social needs of the immigrants.

Some of these first organizations, which formed in the 1970s, were organized around one group's religion, social class, or place of origin. As more Indians arrived, however, some groups expanded to encompass all Indians regardless of religion, class, or place of geographic origin. The Sikh community in California, for

The Chicago Tamil Sangam

As the number of immigrants from India grew, it was natural that people from one region of India would settle near those from the same region. By the same measure, tensions that existed between groups from different areas of India were sometimes carried to the United States. In India, one of the main points of contention is whether government policies favor Hindi speakers from northern India or Indians from Tamil Nadu and several other southern Indian states who speak the Tamil language. The Tamil largely follow the Hindu faith, and they share a culture, cuisine, and artistic tradition that are distinctly different from those of northern India. While the early immigrants to the United States considered themselves "Indian," later arrivals defined their background more clearly. This led to the establishment of separate Indian organizations that were based on the immigrants' language and region.

One example of such an organization is Chicago's Tamil Sangam. It began when a group of immigrant Tamils got together regularly to share potluck dinners and talk about their culture. Today the group has grown to more than three hundred members and hosts events attended by more than a thousand people in the Chicago area. It is a formal organization with a constitution, bylaws, elections, a board of directors, and specific activity committees.

The group's primary goals are preserving the Tamil language through language classes and maintaining the Tamil culture. The Tamil Sangam celebrates Indian festivals like Pongal (the New Year) and Divali (a festival of lights to honor the return from exile of the legendary hero Rama). It also hosts an annual Children's Day.

example, established religious and social centers called Gurdwaras that were originally intended for Sikhs only. As more Indians arrived in the 1960s, the Gurdwaras offered shelter, food, and social activities to all immigrants regardless of caste, ethnic origins, or religion.

As the Indian population expanded in many urban areas in the 1980s, some organizations split to reflect the regional, religious, or linguistic diversity of an area's immigrant population. For example, members of the Association of Indians in America began to regroup in order to satisfy their need to express a specific ethnic identity, whether it be Gujarati, Tamilian, or Bengali. In this way, Indians could spend time with others who spoke their language, ate the same kind of food, and dressed the same way.

These organizations sponsored festivals and other events that met a crucial need:

helping Indian immigrants preserve and express their Indian identity. The opportunity to wear traditional garb, especially in public, is important to many Indians because it sends a message that Indian values have not been abandoned. In this regard, the organizations that sponsor such events meet a need that cannot be fulfilled in private. No matter how rigorously Indians adhere to their cultural values at home, most believe that participation in group activity is a key component of Indian tradition.

The importance of these cultural organizations to Indian immigrants is reflected in the numbers who join them: A total of 61 percent who participated in a recent survey said they belonged to an Indian community organization. About 37 percent of Indians have joined regional, cultural, or language-based organizations and 26 percent belong to religious organizations, while 5 percent belong to pan-Indian groups.

Political and Professional Organizations

In addition to sponsoring cultural events, some immigrant organizations provided members with an opportunity to express their interests in a collective voice that gained the attention of local political establishments. In the past, Indians had achieved independence by standing up for their rights, and now they were beginning to see that asserting their political rights could benefit them in the United States as well. One immigrant, Satish, stated, "As you know, Indians have not been treated well in many other parts of the world. In view of that experience we must unite ourselves in this country and protect our rights."[24]

Organizations such as the Indian American Political Forum for Political Action and Indian American Center for Political Awareness worked at first to inform immigrants of their rights and provide legal help related to immigration issues. From there the organizations branched into voter registration drives and the publication of pamphlets that discussed the effect of local issues on the Indian community.

Other organizations, such as the nationwide Network of Indian Professionals, combine political, social, and professional activities. Members of this group are drawn from professions such as medicine, law, engineering, art, and computer technology. They represent, in many ways, the pinnacle of success for both the Indian and American way of life. The group arranges political lobbying, professional development workshops and seminars, and social events to celebrate the members' Indian heritage. To further assist the community, the individual chapters provide scholarships to Indian American students. The group describes its purpose as not only aiding the Indian American community but also increasing overall public awareness of the remarkable intellectual and social contributions made by Indian Americans.

In a sense, this organization represents the next step in the evolution of the second wave of Indian immigrants. While the first Indian organizations were social and cultural, allowing newcomers to socialize with other immigrants and maintain contact with their old traditions, the newer organizations

Many Indian immigrants continue to participate in traditional cultural activities. Here, three Indian dancers prepare for an exhibition.

began to look for ways in which the Indian immigrants could assert their presence and participate in American culture.

Reinforcing Indian Culture

The second wave grew increasingly large by the last decade of the twentieth century. In 1990 the U.S. census reported the Indian American population at 815,447. According to the Population Reference Bureau, the population grew by 103 percent in the decade between 1980 and 1990. As this growing population continues to observe traditional social and religious rituals, it has slowly increased the awareness of many Americans about Indian culture.

In order to bring attention to and celebrate their native culture, many Indian immigrants participate in or attend exhibitions of traditional Indian arts, including

dance and music. In Chicago, the classical Indian dance school Bharatanatyam keeps alive three-thousand-year-old traditions from South India. The dancers interpret Hindu scriptures through body and movements, rhythm, and facial expressions. This form of dance offers a path that brings both dancers and audience closer to a spiritual awareness.

At the same time, some immigrants attempt to incorporate aspects of both Indian and American culture. For example, another classical Indian dance is *kathak*, from North India, which evolved from ancient traditions in entertaining Indian royalty. *Kathak* is accompanied by vocals and percussion. At the Natyakalayalam Dance Company, director Hema Rajagopalan strives to mix classical dance styles with innovations that reflect the new environment of the immigrant. Rajagopalan says that her students have many reasons for dancing, including to seek release from the pressures of living an immigrant life, to search for an ethnic identity, and to gain a better understanding of self.

In general, much of the organization of religious festivals, cultural shows, parades, and other events has fallen to women. Part of the reason that Indian women have become so involved in these events is that they have been torn from their role in the extended family that they knew in India. In addition, differences between American and Indian values, especially ideas about friendship, at times make it difficult for women to develop close personal relationships with Americans. India scholar G.U. Coelho describes a typical Indian friendship:

Much of the responsibility for preserving native Indian culture falls to women. This young woman teaches two students to perform kathak, *a classical Indian dance.*

Three major values are assumed to exist in the mature Indian friendship. First, friendship represents a close interdependence and interlocking of needs and interests. The question of undue interference in each other's affairs or insensitivity to each other's privacy does not seriously arise. A second basic assumption . . . is that there is always time to reciprocate favors and benefits. A third basic assumption is that a friendship cannot, or rather may not be broken. Indian friendship is a life-long commitment.[25]

Friendships in America, on the other hand, do not necessarily conform to these values. For example, most Americans strongly value their privacy. So when Indian women immigrants leave their lifelong circle of friends and family, they often fill that void in other ways, such as organizing cultural events. In a sense, organizing such events has helped many women emerge into a new type of social role, one that combines Indian and American customs. Many immigrant Indian women have come to enjoy a freedom in the United States that was not available to them in India. One immigrant woman said, "Coming to America has enhanced my life, broadened my thinking. In India I would not have matured the way I have. I would have been less exposed."[26]

Cultural Confusion

While women's roles in fostering the growing visibility of Indian culture have benefited both immigrants and interested Americans, the change in the role of women from first-generation to second-generation immigrants has created tension within their population. With women's slow adaptation to the American norm, the traditional Indian purdah is violated. This Hindi word literally means "veil" or "curtain," but in Indian culture it refers to the practice of keeping women isolated from life outside the home. Writer Hannah Papanek explains, "In a purdah society, women are simultaneously defined as being very important in the family unit and very vulnerable when they move into the world outside home."[27]

As their roles changed in the United States, however, that mix of importance and vulnerability trapped many women between the past and present. Complicating matters was the fact that even as first-generation women attempted to raise their children according to traditional Indian values, those values themselves were changing in India as it slowly entered the modern world. Sociologist Sathi Dasgupta says the first-generation Indian American women presented an older picture of India—the one in which they were raised. According to Dasgupta, "the attitudes of Indians long settled in the U.S. have frozen in time."[28]

Gender Division

Nowhere were such rigid attitudes more apparent than in the debate about marriage in the Indian community. The expectation that young men and women would marry within the Indian community remained unchanged. Yet second-generation Indian Americans experienced a divide between traditional gender roles and modern Indian American attitudes.

The result of this cultural confusion was that young women of the second generation found that as much as they admired Indian tradition, they were unable to find an Indian man who supported their American independence, assertiveness, activism, and ambition. As the second generation reached marriage age, many young Indian American men returned to their parents' homelands in India to find traditional brides. This had the effect of producing a division in the second generation about women's roles. This division resulted between Indian American women who had grown up in the more liberated America and women of the same age raised in a more cloistered, traditional Indian upbringing.

As roles for women change in both the United States and India, Indian American mothers like this woman find it difficult to raise children in accordance with traditional values.

Links to the Homeland

In spite of their newfound freedom in the United States, most immigrant women—and men—profess a profound devotion to their homeland in India. Many still feel strong emotional ties to India and a sense of longing and obligation toward faraway relatives. According to one Chicago survey, more than 78 percent of Indian immigrants professed to be "very attached" or "somewhat attached" to their homeland.

One way immigrants stay linked to their homeland is by following the media on local and national happenings in India. Many immigrants subscribe to newspapers and magazines that focus on Indian issues. In major metropolitan areas, such as New York and Chicago, immigrants can even watch Indian programs broadcast on television.

Most immigrants remain in close contact—through letters, phone calls, and e-mail—with family members left in India. Many immigrant families manage to visit India every two to three years. They go to revitalize ties with parents, grandparents, aunts, uncles, and cousins. They also go to formally recognize any changes in the family, such as deaths, births, or marriages, since they were last in India. Such observance could entail praying for a deceased uncle at the local temple or bestowing blessings, affection, and gifts on the newest niece.

Some immigrants return regularly to India whether or not they have close relatives to visit. For these individuals, the sense of belonging to a familiar culture—even one that is changing with the time—brings peace and tranquility they rarely feel in the United States. One immigrant woman says that visiting India provides a sense of comfort:

Isolation or Cultural Preservation?

This immigrant, quoted in Sathi S. Dasgupta's book On the Trail of an Uncertain Dream, *discusses why he isolates himself from American culture and feels more comfortable participating in Indian culture:*

I don't go to restaurants and movies here, because I don't like the movies here, nor do I enjoy American food. I enjoy going to movies and restaurants when I visit India. Here, the nature of my boredom is different. In India, when I used to sit on the porch and watch people, I used to feel that though they are not my friends and I don't know them, they are my "people." But here when I see people coming and going, I don't feel anything. Like if there is some accident somewhere and somebody gets hurt, I would go and help and then forget about him. But in India, I would feel curious as to who he is. Where does he live? What happened to him afterwards? But here I feel completely blank.

Even when I travel from the north to the south in India, I never feel lonely. There's a sense of belonging, you can never get it here [in the United States]. Going to the temple here is not quite the same as going to the temple in India. It has to be planned; the temples are forty miles away. In India, I don't have to make sure my kids are okay, that one of them doesn't have a test the next morning, the other doesn't have a fever, that my husband doesn't have music practice, that he is available to take us in the car. In India, the atmosphere is different. You can hear the bells ringing, you can see the temple up on the hillock, and you have a bath and take a walk down and say your prayers. My boys would just go and do a *shastang pranam* (prostrate themselves in prayer) at the temple, and everyone else would be doing it. It is never the same in America—it can't be. You have to tell yourself, you have to do this or that. In India, nobody has to tell you, you just do it. The need to define one's identity is not there. It just *is*.[29]

Aid to India

For many immigrants, attachment to the homeland is expressed through the spirit of giving from afar. Doing something to help those less fortunate in India is a popular goal among Indian immigrants in America. Many immigrants feel that they have some mission in life beyond family and self, a mission that involves aiding those in India.

One immigrant who feels this connection to India strongly is Om Dutt Sharma, a sixty-five-year-old taxi driver in New York City. For twenty years, Sharma and his wife, Krishna, a nurse, saved every dollar they could spare so they could spend twenty-five hundred dollars each year to run a small school for 180 little girls in his native village in India. In addition, the Sharmas spend five hundred dollars annually to pay a local doctor to give the girls regular medical checkups.

To support India, national organizations such as the Association for India's Development were formed. This nonprofit organization has thirty-six chapters across the United States whose mission is to raise funds to support social development projects to improve the lives of poor and underprivileged people in India. The organization pays tribute to the Indian values of peace and justice.

The Role of Religion

While maintaining some form of contact with the homeland is very important for many Indian immigrants, religion seems to play varying roles in their lives. Many immigrants say that religion became more important for them after they came to the United States. Even for immigrants who are not religious, their faith—whatever it might be—serves as a link to social and cultural traditions of India. For example, Ram, who came to the United States in 1990, does not consider himself particularly religious, but he participates in at least six religious festivals at home and in the community each year because he believes the activities help

The Hindu Religion

Hinduism is the world's oldest faith still in existence. There are nearly 1 billion Hindus worldwide, mostly in India and other parts of Asia. Unlike many other major world religions, Hinduism does not follow a sacred text or the teaching of a single founder. For Hindus, their faith is as much a way of life as it is a religion.

Hindus believe that all genuine religions lead to the same spiritual path and worship the same supreme God. However, Hindus worship God in several forms, both masculine and feminine, in order to understand God better. The masculine forms of God are Brahma (the creator), Vishnu (the protector), and Shiva (the destroyer and re-creator). The feminine forms of God include Shakti or Durga (provider of energy and power), Lakshmi (provider of prosperity and wealth), and Saraswathi (provider of knowledge and intelligence).

Hindus also adhere to basic principles that guide their way of life. One principle is a belief in nonviolence, which is the basis for their vegetarian diet. Another belief is karma, or the law of cause and effect, which means that the good that people do in life will come back to them and the bad they do will also return. Hindus also believe in reincarnation, meaning that every person's soul returns to Earth several times in a new life. The purpose of the cycle of rebirth is for the person to achieve better karma each time, until the soul is purified. Once purification is achieved, the soul is freed from the cycle of rebirth and lives with God for eternity.

Indian American women celebrate the Hindu New Year in a Philadelphia temple.

to maintain his Indian identity. Ram's home includes a small Hindu altar, where his wife frequently prays. He and his family visit the nearest temples on occasion.

Like Ram, many immigrants are less influenced by the dogma of their religion than by the ties it represents to the Indian culture. As the birthplace of two of the world's largest religions, Hinduism and Buddhism, India has a long religious history. Before emigrating, Indian Americans did not have to make an effort to infuse their lives with religion because in their homeland, religion is everywhere, in the media, at the market, in street processions, at family gatherings, and at home.

Once in the United States, they had to create a religious environment where one did not previously exist. This effort has grown in importance as Indian Americans have spread across the United States and found themselves isolated. This link to a cultural identity through religion also became important as a way of educating their children in Indian culture. Parents take their children to Indian festivals, parades, and temples, and encourage them to pray at home altars and participate in family religious activities in order to create an environment for their children filled with Indian traditions.

Indian traditions include not only such cultural attributes as food, clothing, dance, and music, but also values that immigrants feel set Indians apart from mainstream America. Parents hope that by infusing Indian traditions and values into their children's lives they can counteract what they consider to be dangerous influences in American society, such as television and movies.

While the effort to offer children a link to Indian culture has succeeded in instilling Indian values in this second generation, it has not entirely shielded them from American culture. This has resulted in a generation of Indian Americans who are struggling to find their identities as both Indian and American while at the same time remaining respectful of their parents. This evolution of the immigrant culture has become an ongoing struggle for the new generation of Indian Americans.

CHAPTER SIX

Between Two Worlds

Most of the children of the Indian immigrants who began arriving in the 1960s were born in the United States. The few who immigrated with their parents were mostly very young (under the age of five years) and have little if any memory of life in India. For this second generation of Indian Americans, who are known as *desi*, growing up in the United States has presented a different set of challenges from those their parents faced.

In general, the second generation has had a more difficult time than their parents in being American at school or work and Indian at home. Often, cultural confusion results from being asked to follow one set of values at home and another in society at large. The children of the second generation perceive a conflict between the different expectations of their behavior in these two roles and often target their parents as the cause of this conflict. Twenty-year-old Anar Nagar, an American-born daughter of Indian immigrants, describes this conflict with her mother:

Sometimes I go talk to [my mother] . . . tell her about how I want to go to med school. And she's just like, "Well, you know, the most important thing is raising a family." And I'm just

Parental Conflicts

Indian youth and their immigrant parents disagree on many issues besides dating. For girls, in particular, disagreement over relatively unimportant matters can deepen into conflict that pits Indian customs against modern American society. Anar Nagar explains one such issue in Jean Bacon's book Life Lines: Community, Family, and Assimilation Among Asian Indian Immigrants.

It was implicit sometimes. Just the way they talked about what they felt was beautiful, or attractive. Like with my hair. They thought the most beautiful hair was long and straight, and parted in the middle. . . . I didn't like it. But that was still the most beautiful thing to them. Every time I would talk about getting my hair cut or pointing out a hairstyle that I liked, they'd be like, "That's not pretty!" And things like, "We're the ones that have to look at you. It doesn't matter what you think is attractive. . . ." It was pretty traumatizing sometimes. . . . They would take my curling iron away. Or they wouldn't let me buy hair spray. So I'd end up taking my makeup to school or curling my hair at someone else's house. Just so I wouldn't have to cause tension in the house and still get away with what I wanted.

like, "What're you talking about?! You know, like my career comes first." . . . It just surprises me. But . . . that's something that she really believes. . . . It's really confusing, the messages are confusing.[30]

The confusion Anar speaks of is common among the children of immigrants. Its emergence in the growing Indian American community has forced the younger generation to redefine what it means to be an Indian in the United States.

Source of Conflict

That redefinition has evolved as the circumstances in the immigrant community have changed. While parents have generally approved of the American educational system and their children have generally excelled in school, many older Indian Americans feel they must go to great lengths to counteract what they see as bad influences at school.

Although many of these concerns are shared by all parents, especially as their kids reach adolescence, many Indian American parents strongly disapprove of what they see as unlimited socialization between boys and girls in the United States. Many are reluctant to allow their children to attend dances or go on dates, equating these behaviors with what they view as uniquely American problems of AIDS, promiscuity, and drugs. In this way, the Indian parents' view of American adolescence exacerbates the normal tensions that exist between virtually all teenagers and their parents.

Indian young people of the second generation find it frustrating that while their parents strongly support getting a good education, they refuse to acknowledge the social aspects of the American educational experience. Indian teens spend their days at school interacting with peers whose parents do not usually oppose dances, dating, and other common activities of American teenagers. Indian teens also spend time in extracurricular activities, such as sports, the arts, and jobs, where they are again exposed to peer pressure and conflicting values.

Many Indian youth want their parents to recognize that they cannot be just like Indian children who are growing up in India. They want their parents to understand that the second generation must change their

A young Indian American woman socializes with male students. Second generation teenagers often clash with their parents about social activities like co-ed dances.

social behavior in order to succeed in an American world.

Yet rather than understand the tension, many Indian parents strengthen their efforts to combat American influences with visits to religious temples, celebration of festivals, Indian dance and music, summer camp, and even special community courses in Indian history and Hindu philosophy. One mother, Alka, explains why she feels this tremendous effort is necessary for her own children: "Raising your child here is different than in India. In India there is an Indian environment; therefore you take it for granted that children will learn [Indian values]. Here it is not so; you have to make conscious efforts so that your children learn some basic values of Indian culture."[31] Although many youth enjoy some exposure to their ethnic heritage, a great number also feel as if Indian culture is being forced on them.

Two Sets of Values

Many members of the second generation consider the necessity of being American at school and Indian at home as hypocrisy. While their parents accepted the contradicting dual roles as part of their immigrant experience, young second-generation Indian Americans are less willing to do so. Many want to accept a mixture of both as a valid identity for themselves. A college student's ideas about his identity reflect this need to accept both roles as a single identity:

If I were to describe myself, I'd say, I was raised with Indian values but my behavior patterns are American. So I think I'm both Indian and American. I wouldn't try to characterize myself as either one. I get values from both sides, but my sense of duty, it's definitely Hinduism. In Hinduism, your sense of duty is stressed more. I personally owe America more for what I am today because I was raised here. I feel pride in both countries but ultimately, if I had to choose, I'd choose America because I feel I owe them more for what I am.[32]

Likewise, second-generation Indian Americans feel pressure to conform to two sets of values. In a sense, parents are asking their children to duplicate their own behavior as a first-generation immigrant— well-behaved, studious, and obedient. Indian parents want their children to consult their family on important decisions and to defer to the parents' opinion when there is a disagreement. As one mother stated, "The children can make their own decisions but we have to guide them. We have to define the choices for them. If my daughter wants to be a fashion model, there is no way I'll allow that."[33]

Yet parents also want their children to be independent, because most realize that success in American schools and workplaces requires assertiveness that would be unacceptable at home. As one parent said, "My children should depend on us but should be independent outside."[34] Again, this echoes the conflict many first-generation Indians faced.

For many *desi*, this adolescent conflict is heightened after leaving school because, according to Indian custom, most Indian youth live with their parents even after graduating from college. Thus, parents play a significant role in the development of their children's identities as Indian Americans even after these children have become young adults. Nevertheless, the children of Indian immigrants often complain that their parents do not understand their difficulties in resolving the contradictions they encounter between school and home—and, after graduation, between work and home.

Pressure to Succeed

Other conflicts arise from parental pressure to achieve, which often begins early in the lives of Indian American youth. Many are asked not only to get good grades, but often to get perfect grades and stay at the top of their classes in every subject. In addition, they are expected to excel in nonsports, nonart types of extracurricular activities, such as debate, journalism, science clubs, and foreign language groups. Many Indian teens feel frustrated under the weight of this pressure to achieve, especially when they do well in school, but fall just short of perfect. Such pressure leaves them feeling overwhelmed, depressed, or resentful.

One reason Indian parents push their children to be so achievement-oriented is that they equate academic success with economic stability. Such stability, in turn, is perceived by first-generation Indians as a good way to fight the stigma of being a minority. An immigrant father who succeeded in his occupation explains this reasoning:

When we first moved to this neighborhood, we were the only non-white family in this neighborhood. At first people used to ignore us, the kids used to make fun of us. But some people from my company live in this neighborhood and when the people around here came to know of my position in my company, they started associating with us. Then everybody started to mix with us.[35]

While many *desi* are raised to act independently and, as such, want to make their own career choices, again there may be parental pressure to enter lucrative fields such as medicine, engineering, and computer science. Further, Indian youth sometimes feel that they are expected to choose careers that will enhance the family's social status.

Of course, Indian youth choose to deal with this situation in varying ways, from mute acceptance to outright defiance. Some give in to parental demands, eventually becoming doctors, engineers, and scientists. Others give up trying to please their parents after attempting such programs in college and finding that they cannot be happy in any of the fields their parents select for them. One student, who wanted to be a teacher, was pressured into taking engineering courses. After a year and a half, however, he disliked engineering strongly and changed his major to education, despite his parents' disapproval. One Indian youth described the disappointment his parents felt at his career choice and his response to this dilemma:

My parents want me to succeed so they can brag about me. Even in the field I'm in, I make decent money, I can survive, I feel happy. But they don't like the fact that I didn't get my Master's or do engineering. Some of the things I do I'm very proud of, but they never brag about that stuff. It took me awhile to have enough self-esteem to say, "I don't care."[36]

Other Indian youth try to compromise between their own goals and their parents' plans for them. They try to fulfill their own needs while meeting their parents' expectations, as biology student Minakshi Kumar explains:

I have different dreams and ambitions for myself. According to me they might be good ideas . . . but to my parents . . . it's not going to be that great to them. If I wanted to . . . excel in drama, or playwriting, or something like that, they would be like, "That's nothing. Anybody could

Like this college student, many second-generation Indian Americans are high achievers, pressured by their parents to excel at school.

do that." Because to them, anything in the sciences is great. . . . Hopefully I'll get a [biology] career, and part-time I can do exactly what I want to do. Writing, directing, or something. I feel that's where my talent lies. . . . I want to make my parents happy, too. 'Cause they've done a lot for me, sacrificed a lot for me. . . . After you have a secure job, you can do anything you want to do, part-time, on the side, as a hobby. That was very good advice. I think it's better this way, for security and a job, as well as pursue your interests.[37]

The Generation Gap

As second-generation Indian immigrants reach adulthood, many are coming to understand that the source of tension between them and their parents is the result of two distinct outlooks on life in the United States. The first generation of Indian Americans is caught between two worlds. They came to America seeking comfort and security, yet they remain nostalgic for the India they left behind.

On the other hand, *desi* born and brought up in the United States do not necessarily experience this conflict. Their only knowledge of the immigrant experience is what they learn from their parents. Although they struggled as teens with the conflict between their parents' idealized attitudes of Indian culture and their own Indian American experience, as young adults many seem to have evolved attitudes that are distinctly modern. They are comfortable with choosing from the best of both worlds. Much of the generation gap results from the fact that *desi* are comfortable creating a new Indian American identity, and the older generation is not.

Contributing to the gap is the fact that most *desi* see their ethnicity from a different angle than their parents do. Immigrants who arrived or who grew up in the United States in the 1960s faced discrimination and other difficulties because there were so few Indians. Attitudes toward Indians have softened because the United States today is more diverse, multicultural, and open than the America that Indian American parents entered. Yet many parents, in the opinion of the young people, still look at American life from the perspective of the 1960s and 1970s. While discrimination still exists, it is less blatant than that encountered by earlier immigrants. In addition, laws now offer immigrants the rights to fight back against discrimination. Yet for all the change, many first-generation Indian Americans remain hostage to their first impressions. Preeta Bansal, the chief lawyer for the state of New York, explains her frustration with the gap that has arisen:

I am struck . . . by the fear and rigidity of some first generation Indian Americans and community groups. The first generation has achieved an unprecedented level of economic success in this country, but we must not be content to retreat behind the walls of the suburban castles we have built, and instead must now focus on building bridges with the rest of society.[38]

The *Desi* Scene

A popular social arena for a great number of Indian American teenagers and young adults is the so-called desi *scene, which is dominated by bhangra remix music, a combination of Indian folk and American dance music. Desi parties are often held at clubs, restaurants, and on college campuses. Desi parties are popular because young Indians can socialize in a setting that blends aspects of Indian and American culture. In a sense, the mix of the two types of music represents the mixing of their two worlds—Indian and American. In the* desi *scene traditional Indian culture successfully combines with what is "cool" in the mainstream youth subculture. Sunaina Marr Maira, a postgraduate anthropology student, describes a* desi *scene in her book* Desis in the House: Indian American Youth Culture in New York City:

Shoulders shrug and arms flail in semblances of bhangra moves, here, far from the wheat fields of the Punjab. . . . Tonight, most faces are various shades of South Asian, but a few African Americans and White folks are getting down on the dance floor too, for this is one of the few . . . nights that draws a noticeably racially mixed crowd. . . . [There are] women in hip-huggers twisting their arms in movements learned partly from Hindi films and partly from other bhangra nights like this. . . . A turbaned Sikh man leaps onto the stage . . . spinning and bouncing with acrobatic, breakdance-like agility. Jumping back into the crowd, he is joined by another young Sikh man, and as the crowd parts in a rapt circle, the two dance around each other in exuberantly coordinated precision. Then three young women who have various degrees of classical dance training step up to the circle, their fluid body movements evoking various genres of Indian dance, "filmi" and folk, and challenging what has been up to now an exclusively male, Punjabi performance.

Questioning Authority

The gap between first- and second-generation Indian Americans has resulted, in many cases, in *desi* questioning the wisdom of their parents, a distinctly non-Indian practice. Second-generation Indians have begun to doubt their parents' true understanding of American culture and are thus reluctant to accept parental judgments without question.

Indian youth perceive American social behavior differently than their parents do. One reason, *desi* think, is that, as part of the original Indian immigrant community, their parents are isolated from mainstream

American society. The second generation feels that their parents have not fully kept pace either with their new country or, in fact, with the more modern family dynamics of India that differ from their parents' childhood upbringing there. As a result, many children complain of the conservative point of view that their parents attempt to instill in them. A second-generation youth said that his father "totally underestimated the effect the American culture would have on [his children]. He thought he'd keep us totally isolated and Indian—like Indian kids were like twenty years ago."[39]

In addition, many Indian youth question whether their parents recognize the changes that have taken place in society over the course of the second wave of immigration. For example, women today, both in India and America, are more independent than ever before. Some *desi* believe that their parents do not acknowledge this. Anar Nagar is a college student who is frequently praised by her mother for being a "good girl" at home—meaning Anar fulfills her duty as a child and as a female, being obedient at all times. However, Anar is uncomfortable with the praise she receives for her "good" behavior because she does not believe that as a female in either American or Indian society she should have to be submissive to anyone.

Standing Up for Themselves

Many Indian youth believe that the demands their parents place on them regarding social behavior and achievement are simply ways to assert control. Despite the pressure to accede to their parents' wishes,

members of the second generation are increasingly standing up to their parents. High school student Veena Shankar describes the stand she took to combat her parents' resistance to her becoming a cheerleader:

> We argued for . . . months. The answer was no, and they said "if you want to do sports, that's fine, but pom-poms is not respectable . . . we don't like you wearing those little short skirts and performing for people." And I said, you know, everything I do in school is academic. I was on the math team, I was on the newspaper. I said that I want something fun, and social, and something where I can use my body. Not my brain. So, finally, my dad, [and] I argued so much that they get to a point with me where it's like, "Well, there's no changing your mind. So, fine, go ahead." They got used to the idea, but not once did they ever come see me perform.[40]

Stories like Veena's are not unusual, as more and more young Indian Americans reject their parents' ideas in favor of their own. While the pain of parental disapproval can be sharp, many report that with time they were able to accept their differences with their parents and felt happier with themselves because they were no longer trying to be two different persons—Indian and American—in two different settings. They were simply taking what they appreciated from both cultures and combining everything into one set of values they could live by.

Other Indians who have reached their twenties simply inform their parents they are doing things differently rather than argue with them. These young adults try to open a line of communication with their parents, showing that they understand and respect their parents' opinions, but that they are old enough to make their own decisions, whether their parents approve or not. Anar Nagar decided to be open with her mother about her male friends at college, although she knew her mother would disapprove:

My friend Dave wanted to come down and spend three days here. She's like, "Uh, no. . . . you two would be here alone when Mausami [Anar's sister] and I aren't home." And I'm just like, "Mom . . . I see him all the time at school. You're never around. He comes into my apartment." Then she just gave me the look, like, whoa. And then the next day she's like, "He comes over to your apartment? No, that's not right. . . . Things can happen." . . . But, then, I'm not interested in him, and I'm trying to explain everything to her. And then I ended up saying something like, "I understand that you feel that way, but I don't agree." And that just ended it right there. That was like the first time I took my stand, different than hers. . . . I was sick of . . . leading this double life, you know. I'm trying to develop a solid view of who I am, and to constantly . . . say one thing and do the other, or hide [hinders that].[41]

Dating and Marriage Issues

As Anar's example indicates, one of the most volatile issues between immigrant parents and their children is social behavior with the opposite sex. The very notion of unchaperoned dating among high school and college students goes against many parents' traditional upbringing. Adding to their concern are the modern social ills that are constantly under the media spotlight and that concern most parents: AIDS, drug abuse, sexual activity, and unwanted pregnancies.

American-born Indian youth are part of their culture, not apart from it. They have grown up with belly piercing, rock concerts, and co-ed college dorms. They have grown up in front of the TV screen and, thanks to talk shows, they accept the premise that few topics in American culture are hidden or taboo. Nothing, however, could be further from the attitudes of their parents. For example, many believe that sex and dating are not appropriate to discuss, much less engage in.

In addition to the view that dating is virtually sexual promiscuity, many first-generation parents worry that dating may negatively affect their children's grades. Some feel that American teenagers spend far too much time engaging in social activities and that they should be more serious about their studies.

However, many Indian youth attribute this attitude to outdated perceptions that further isolate them, and their parents, from American culture. In fact, one fifteen-year-old boy said that dating in the United States was really only "a process of getting acquainted with another person [and is not always about being] boyfriend and girlfriend."[42] Like many Indian youth, he valued social interaction with his friends outside the Indian community and did not agree with his parents' views about dating.

Some immigrant parents are concerned that their son or daughter may end up marrying someone who is not Indian. These parents worry about the conflicts that can arise when people from two cultures

Dating is an issue about which Indian American youth and their parents often disagree. Accepted American practices usually clash with parents' traditional values.

Young Indian Americans generally believe in marriage based on love. Their parents, however, typically prefer arranged marriages.

marry and then disagree about such crucial issues as the religion and upbringing of their children. However, many in the second generation do not see such conflicts as insurmountable in a marriage. One Indian youth said, "I think [parents] should realize that no matter who we date or who we choose to marry, we will always be the same person that we always were."[43]

Generally, second-generation Indians consider the choice of a spouse the same way other Americans do—as a decision to be made between a man and a woman only. However, their parents often see marriage in the traditional Indian manner as an arranged partnership between two families. They feel that it is their right to at least have their opinions and desires respected regarding their children's marriages. While some Indian youth still consent to arranged marriages, others compromise by allowing their parents to choose a potential spouse for them, but deciding themselves whether or not to marry that person after several meetings. However, a growing number of Indian youth feel that they should be allowed—and trusted—to decide whom to marry on their own. Moreover, they are upset that their parents would choose a spouse based on social and economic status rather than personality. One Indian youth explores the reasons for this departure from his parents' views: "Are we corrupt? Or do we look at the situation from a new, different perspective? . . . Obviously, there must be some reason for this path of thinking. We aren't just crazy. It's that we've been exposed to new ideas."[44]

As the second generation comes of age and forges an identity as Indian American, the way Indian immigrants deal with American society will change. As the children of immigrants take over the communities their parents have built, the tradition of isolation from the outside world will weaken and the values of both cultures will continue to mix.

CHAPTER SEVEN

Into the American Mainstream

For many Indians who came to the United States in the 1960s and subsequent decades, a lingering question was how much—or even whether—to assimilate into the American mainstream. Increasingly, however, immigrants now think of themselves not as Indians but as Indian Americans. With this gradual shift in outlook has come an awareness of the need to take a more active role in the cultural and political life of their adopted home. Scholar Jean Bacon sums up this transformation:

> as the immigrants approached middle age and their children approached adulthood, [Indian] community members began to view themselves as permanent residents rather than sojourners. They began . . . to establish political, professional, and cultural outreach organizations to improve the condition of the Indian community within the larger society.[45]

Apathy and Disunity

According to the 1990 U.S. census, more than 34 percent of the 593,423 Indian immigrants in the United States had been naturalized and were therefore able to vote. In addition, more than 212,000 Indian Americans had been born in the

United States and therefore were citizens. By the year 2000, the population had grown to almost 1.7 million, making the Indian American community a potentially formidable voting force.

However, prior to 2000, very few Indian Americans exercised their right to vote, and only a handful attempted to participate in the political process by seeking elective office. With the exception of Dalip Singh's term as California senator in the 1950s, the highest elective offices held by Indian Americans are those of Kumar Barve, a Maryland State Assembly delegate, Swati Dandekar, Iowa State Assembly delegate, and Satveer Chowdhry, a Minnesota State Assembly delegate.

Traditionally, Indian Americans have been most politically involved through their campaign contributions. Many have been very active in fundraising for political candidates on the federal, state, and local levels. The funds raised go to those candidates whom the community perceives as

An Indian American woman (right) and other immigrants take the citizenship oath. Despite their large numbers, few Indian Americans exercise their right to vote.

best suited to represent its views, usually regardless of their party. The fact that Indian Americans have a history of crossing party lines keeps politicians of both major parties actively courting their vote through organizations such as the Indian American Forum for Political Education. This organization holds annual seminars at which many senators, representatives, and other elected officials are invited to speak.

Despite these and many other opportunities to connect with the Indian American community, some Indian Americans complain that political candidates take their money but fail to support Indian American interests in a meaningful way. In 1995, for example, the American Association of Physicians of Indian Origin (AAPI) raised funds for President Bill Clinton's reelection campaign by hosting a dinner at which the president spoke. More than 120 members contributed one thousand dollars apiece to attend the dinner. Clinton's speech, however, turned out to be a short address in which he vaguely reiterated his plans for health care reform and his intentions to involve Indian American physicians in those plans. The noncommittal speech left many AAPI physicians incensed that they had received nothing tangible in return for their contributions.

Another problem Indian Americans perceive about their community is that their political views are far from unified under any ethnic, religious, or social class umbrella. Although Democrats have a two-to-one advantage over Republicans among Indians who do have a political preference, a 2002 survey indicated that four in ten Indians refuse to label themselves as either liberal or conservative. Interestingly, this

"Stand Up and Take Notice": Indian Americans in Political Office

In 2002 more Indian Americans than ever before ran for elective office, including one, Venkat Challa of North Carolina, who made a bid for the U.S. Senate. Of the thirty candidates, whose bids ranged from local to national office, only three won their campaigns. Still, the Indian American community was encouraged because so many made the effort.

In addition to Challa's lost bid for the Senate, three Indian Americans lost races for the House of Representatives. However, two were reelected to their state assemblies —Kumar Barve in Maryland and Satveer Chowdhry in Minnesota. Confident of the political future for Indian Americans, Varun Nikore of the Indian American Leadership Incubator said, "These wins . . . are further proof that Indian Americans, in particular, are viable. It should be a signal to the [political] party structures, who often create impediments for candidates new to the system, that they should stand up and take notice of the rising surge of Asian American candidates."

indifference carries over into politics in India as well. A majority of Indians in the same survey said they did not care which political party led the Indian government.

Some politically active Indian Americans note that the tendency for organizations to concentrate on cultural issues has overshadowed the importance of politics. Ranjit Ganguly, a founder of the Indo-American Democratic Organization (IADO), complains, "Indians are only keen on cultural extravaganzas, they are not interested in issue-oriented politics. . . . They don't realize that if you don't organize politically, you don't exist, at least in the eyes of the government."[46]

Creating a Political Identity
It is this lack of unity that prompted some Indian Americans to organize groups like the Indo-American Democratic Organization. The IADO began in 1980 when a few members of the Indian community in Chicago realized that without political cohesion, the local authorities would ignore their needs. Over two decades, IADO membership has swelled to more than five hundred members, IADO has initiated numerous programs, such as registering thousands of Indian Americans to vote conducting candidate forums working on numerous local, state, and federal office campaigns and campaigning against media stereotypes and hate crimes. Its members serve on various Asian advisory committees at the state and local levels and have been appointed as delegates from Illinois to the Democratic National Convention. As a result, Chicago's political candidates actively seek the support of IADO. However, IADO still seeks ways to get the ethnic community more involved politically by building an awareness of important issues through educational seminars. In all of its outreach and lobbying, IADO has become a model for an increasing number of similar Indian American organizations in other regions of the United States.

Hate Crimes
In recent years, Indian Americans have begun to realize the importance of asserting their presence. As the Indian community has become more visible as a distinct social and cultural group within the United States, it has had to face some serious problems, including job discrimination and racial attacks.

Indian Americans have gradually realized that being an economically successful model minority is not enough to protect their rights. For example, in 1994, a rash of hate crimes was perpetrated against the Indian community in the New York–New Jersey area, a total of sixteen incidents of racial violence within two months. The following year, the same region reported four fatal racial attacks on Indian American businessmen.

The intensity of this violence grew immensely after the terrorist attacks on New York City and Washington, D.C., on September 11, 2001. Although no one of Indian descent was to blame, more than three hundred Indian Americans were attacked in the week after September 11—a number equal to the number of such crimes reported over a normal six-month period in the United

An Indian girl and her father mourn the victims of the September 11, 2001, terrorist attacks. In the aftermath of the attacks, hate crimes against Indian Americans increased.

States. Among those crimes were the murder of a Sikh gas station owner in Arizona, a man in New York City who was shot in the forehead by a BB gun as he left a temple, and a Virginia man who was forced off the road by two vans on his way to donate blood. In Boston, Massachusetts, three Indian American college students were attacked and beaten by white teenagers, who called them "son of Osama Bin Laden." Across the United States, hate crimes rose by more than 40 percent after September 11.

A Network of Organizations

With the increase in hate crimes both before and after September 11, the Indian American community organized to create a network of websites that affirms its rights and alerts the community to issues that concern it. Action-India is a website where Indians can inform public officials and elected representatives about the Indian community's views. Info-India monitors the media in order to improve the quality and quantity of reporting of news that affects the Indian community. These sites and many others have helped to unite Indian Americans all over the United States, building an awareness of the need for political action if the community's concerns are to be heard by the government.

Another operation developed to meet the political needs of the Indian American community is the Congressional Caucus on India and Indian Americans. The caucus, which was formed in 1993 and now has more than one hundred members, serves as a lobbying group that brings the attention of Congress to issues relating to Indian Americans. Former Democratic cochair Gary Ackerman explained that the goals of the caucus are carried out through "task forces devoted to immigration, international trade, U.S. economic sanctions in India, international terrorism and other issues of concern to the Indian-American community."[47]

Other lobbying efforts of the caucus address domestic issues such as education, minority businesses, immigration and family reunion, political empowerment of the ethnic community, and health and human services. With the increased need for attention to Indian American rights after September 11, however, some politically involved Indian Americans think that the caucus is falling short of meeting its goals. Complaints about the lack of meetings among members, the failure to circulate news articles or reports on issues, and a general lack of focus and organization are common. There are also specific groups of Indian Americans that have identified legislative agendas at the national level, including the Indus Entrepreneurs and the American Association of Physicians of Indian Origin.

Contribution to Literature

While political involvement for most Indian Americans is limited, their contributions to the arts and sciences are exploding. Literature, film, and music, as well as scientific and technological research, have become hallmarks of the Indian American success story.

Indian as well as Indian American writers are producing some of the best-selling literature available. The phenomenon began with the huge success of Indian

With the success of her novel The God of Small Things, *Arundhati Roy became one of the world's most accomplished Indian authors.*

American Bharati Mukherjee, whose books include *The Middleman and Other Stories*, which won the National Book Critics Circle Award in 1988. In the 1990s, Arundhati Roy's novel *The God of Small Things* sparked an interest in Indian culture and issues. This interest has been growing since the extensive publicity in 1997 of the fiftieth anniversary of India's independence. Roy's book sold almost 3 million copies and garnered the coveted British Booker Prize as well as a number of American awards.

Today, a myriad of young Indian writers have been creating literature that gives voice to issues important to first- and second-generation immigrants. Jhumpa Lahiri, the daughter of Bengali immigrants, won a Pulitzer Prize in 2000 for her first book, *Interpreter of Maladies*, a collection of stories that brings to life the complications and confusion of Indian immigrants living in the United States. Best-selling author of *Sister of My Heart*, Chitra Banerjee Divakaruni, explains the important impact of Indian American literature, especially on women:

> We cannot ignore the crucial part played by the growing number of immigrants who read our books because they understand their own communities better since we [second-generation immigrants] write from a perspective that is not available to a writer who has lived in India. . . . But a growing number of American women—who are curious about the foreigners living in their middle—want to read [our] stories too. . . . Many of us articulate in our books

the deepest fear and trauma faced by women in India and here—and show they emerge, at least in many cases, as stronger and self-reliant women. Some of our characters are good role models for women readers and women activists.[48]

In the field of journalism and political writing, Indian American Fareed Zakaria has made a strong impression with his writing on democracy in magazines and newspapers. He has been the managing editor of America's most influential foreign policy publication, *Foreign Affairs*, and a columnist for *Newsweek* magazine. Zakaria has also written on international affairs in the *New York Times*, the *Wall Street Journal*, and the *New Republic*. His 2003 book, *The Future of Freedom*, won strong reviews for its examination of the nature of democracy.

Film and Music Contributions

Indian filmmakers are also making their mark on the American mainstream. Films about the Indian immigrant experience are enjoyed by a wide audience. Mira Nair's feature film *Salaam Bombay* was nominated for Academy Awards in 1988. Her 1992 film *Mississippi Masala* highlighted the lives of Indians living in the Deep South and their somewhat complicated relationships with African Americans. Other Nair films, *The Perez Family* (1995) and *Kama Sutra* (1997), also enjoyed both critical acclaim and wide audiences. The newest behind-the-scenes star in film is M. Night Shyamalan, who wrote and directed blockbuster hits such

The Next Great Hollywood Storyteller

M. Night Shyamalan has been touted as the next Steven Spielberg ever since his thriller, *The Sixth Sense*, impressed moviegoers in 1999. Although his next big feature, *Unbreakable*, succeeded only modestly at the box office, his third film, *Signs* (2002), in which he acted in a minor role, garnered both popular and critical acclaim. At the age of thirty-one, he is one of the highest paid screenwriters

M. Night Shyamalan is one of the most successful filmmakers in Hollywood.

and directors in Hollywood.

Shyamalan was born to Indian immigrant parents. He grew up in the Philadelphia suburbs and attended Catholic schools, although he was raised Hindu. Inspired by the movie *Raiders of the Lost Ark* (1981), Shyamalan began making movies at age ten, using a video camera.

Shyamalan made his first feature film in 1992, an independent venture called *Praying with Anger*, which grossed only $7,000 at the box office. In 1994 he wrote a script called *Labor of Love*, which was purchased by Fox but was never made into a film. Then in 1996 Shyamalan directed his next screenplay, *Wide Awake*. However, due to disagreements about the final editing, this film, too, was never released at the box office (although it was later released on DVD). Finally, the director got his big break with the phenomenal success of *The Sixth Sense*. Shyamalan's achievements in the American movie industry are admired by both Indians and Americans.

as *The Sixth Sense* (1999), *Unbreakable* (2000), and *Signs* (2002), catapulting himself into the realm of the top moviemakers in America.

In addition to literature and films, Indian music, one of the most traditional of all Indian arts, is becoming better known among the American public. The popularity of

Indian music, both traditional and modern, is due mainly to the promotion of traditional styles and modern artists through foundations such as the Association of Performing Arts of India (APAI). The APAI, founded in 1998, offers classes in sitar (a string instrument) and tabla (percussion). It showcases both northern (Hindustani) and southern (Carnatic) traditional music and has presented such artists as Ustad Irshad Khan, a renowned master of the sitar, and vocalist Shubha Mudgal, who has recorded many film soundtracks. Indian artist Ali Akbar Khan, winner of two Grammys and the 1991 MacArthur genius grant, has not only performed all over the world, but has passed on his expertise in Indian classical music to ten thousand students at his Ali Akbar College of Music in San Rafael, California. Winner of the 1999 National Heritage Fellowship, Zakir Hussain has lent a traditional Indian accompaniment to such popular musicians as John McLaughlin, the Grateful Dead, and Van Morrison.

Success in the Sciences

In the fields of science and technology, several Indian Americans have made remarkable contributions. Recognized as one of the most important astrophysicists of the twentieth century, Subramanyan Chandrasekhar produced advanced theories relating to the universe and conducted experiments in nuclear and chemical reactions. NASA's new X-ray observatory, which was launched into space in July 1999, was named *Chandra* in his honor.

Space exploration has had its tragedies. Indian American Kalpana Chawla was one of seven astronauts killed in the *Columbia* space shuttle disaster on February 1, 2003. Born in India, Chawla came to the United States at age twenty to study aeronautical engineering. She became a U.S. citizen and, in 1994, was selected as an astronaut. Chawla will be remembered as having given her life in the quest for scientific knowledge.

In the technology field, Vinod Dham was responsible for creating one of Silicon Valley's most marketable products, the K6 chip. During the 1990s his superior design work on Intel's Pentium computer earned him the name "Father of the Pentium." Today, Pentium computers are used in millions of American households, schools, and businesses.

Sharing India's Heritage

Today Indian Americans are also sharing their talents and heritage through outreach efforts. Outreach is conducted through a variety of means, such as clubs, associations, seminars, and multicultural education. Indian Americans feel a growing willingness to share Indian cuisine, music, dance, festivals, traditional medicine, and many other aspects of their culture with the rest of American society in order to promote greater understanding.

Across the United States, small, local organizations dedicated to sharing Indian culture with the non-Indian population have sprung up, many supported by *desi* or even third-generation Indian Americans who are enjoying renewed pride in their heritage. Many of these organizations are based on college campuses and are facilitated by students. In Corvallis, Oregon, the India Association of Oregon State University boasts a membership of students and families of Indian origin. The India Association presents the heritage of India through organized events to the entire Corvallis community. Oregon State University also is home to the Indian Spiritual Organization, whose purpose is to spread Hindu philosophies and the spiritual way of life as it is practiced in India. This organization does community service work, hosts seminars and lectures given by prominent Indian spiritual leaders, holds regular group meditation meetings, and sponsors open discussions for students on spiritual issues.

In addition to local outreach efforts, many organizations and individuals are dedicated to sharing specific aspects of Indian culture on a national level. Many schools and institutes facilitate student and teacher exchange programs between India and the United States. Others hold classes for professors and scholars all over the world on ancient Indian sciences, arts, and philosophy. Dr. Partap Chauhan spreads the practice of ayurveda, a holistic, natural school of Eastern medicine, to thousands of people through his website, which disseminates free advice, online courses, and holistic medicines.

Embracing America

With the renewed interest in sharing Indian culture with the rest of America have come increased efforts by the Indian American community to learn about, understand, and participate more fully in mainstream American society. Some of these efforts are due to the coming of age of the second generation and its more open acceptance of American culture, but others are a result of the changing needs of the Indian community. This change in thinking is evident in the growing awareness that Indian and American cultures are not complete opposites.

For example, Indian parents are beginning to be aware that the problems posed by sexual activity and drug abuse among teens are concerns not just for them, but for American parents as well.

Indian Americans are starting to see that the American mainstream has something of value to offer the immigrant population. Primarily, they are learning how to better compete in the professional and educational realms. Many Indian professionals are taking seminars offered by various organizations that help them gain insights into American culture that are useful in both work and social settings. The topics covered in such seminars include fashion, handling different types of interaction at work, communicating with government and corporate bureaucracies, and writing effective résumés.

Indian Americans, especially the younger generation, are also participating more in the larger society. Many local, state, and national organizations offer programs for building confidence and assertiveness in young people so they can participate more fully in mainstream society. One such group, Indify, offers a competitive fellowship program to young college graduates and professionals that challenges them to demonstrate an interest in community service both in the United States and in India. It also sponsors a national program in which young Indian professionals serve as mentors and role models to high school students, developing relationships through activities such as outdoor trips, sporting events, and concerts. In many second-generation communities, these activities foster a sense of

U.S.-India Relations

As the Indian population in the United States has grown and become more politically active, there has been a trend toward a greater focus on relations between the United States and India. Indian Americans are concerned not just about what is happening in their homeland, but also about how India's affairs affect the nation to which they immigrated. In particular, Indian Americans have pushed the U.S. government to pay greater attention to economic and national security issues that both countries share. Congressman Benjamin Gilman of New York summed up this relationship at the Congressional Caucus on India and Indian-Americans website:

The relationship between America and India is based on the solid foundation of a shared commitment to democracy, individual rights, freedom of expression and free markets. India offers enormous opportunities for trade and investment for U.S. companies. At the same time, the U.S. and India are confronted by many of the same threats, particularly the forces of international terrorism. India's democratic governing system is a beacon of hope for the region. Close U.S.-India ties will mean a better life for the American and Indian peoples, and a more stable and prosperous world.

India's prime minister and America's president George W. Bush meet in 2001 to discuss their countries' relationship and common goals.

pride and help the students develop leadership skills.

Yet another way Indian Americans participate in mainstream society is through extensive community service, not just for their own ethnic group, but for people of all classes, ethnicities, and religions. In Chicago the Indo-American Center serves the needs of anyone who asks for help, particularly the elderly, the unemployed, and the illiterate. One of its most successful programs helps immigrants to become citizens of the United States. Promoting citizenship has become a major goal for many organizations because without it, individuals cannot participate in the effort to get their needs met. One young Indian American said, "You have to become a citizen if you want a voice in this country. You can't change what you don't like unless you join in."[49] The Indo-American Center offers instruction in English, U.S. history, the Constitution, and government for those who want to become citizens. Like Chicago, many other metropolitan areas with a significant Indian population offer similar services through nonprofit organizations and religious institutions, which are staffed by Indian immigrant volunteers.

From Indian Immigrant to Indian American

Today, more Indian immigrants than ever are giving up their resistance to change. While being Indian is still a very important part of who they are, it does not form their entire identity. Many immigrants, and especially their children, are developing an identity that enables them to adapt to mainstream society. Durga Shenoy, a first-generation immigrant who raised her children in the United States, explains this philosophy:

That's the whole thing about change is that you either change or you die. You perish slowly and steadily. . . . I didn't want my kids to be that way. . . . I wasn't afraid of the change, either. That is, I didn't feel that just because they have learned English language, that they would not be aware of their roots. If . . . they had this burning desire to go back and rediscover their roots . . . that would be their own decision, to do that.[50]

With the dawn of the twenty-first century, Indian immigrants are beginning to embrace something called Indian American culture. Parents are being advised to modify some of the traditional ways of child rearing and to talk more openly with their children about dating and marriage. Many more Indians are adapting their lifestyle to fit the mainstream without sacrificing their cultural heritage. To be Indian American is becoming a positive identity. Dr. Saraswathy Ramanathan, in his description of his naturalization (becoming a citizen), demonstrates how Indian Americans can embrace the new culture without giving up the old:

I am happy to report that after 32 years in the United States, I have finally become an American Citizen. I must admit, I avoided it for many

Today, many Indian Americans embrace life in the United States while preserving their native culture. Here, a woman in traditional dress crosses a street in Chicago's Indian District.

years—I never felt comfortable taking the oath of citizenship—one has to "relinquish any and all allegiance to all foreign sovereigns." . . . But then, reality struck. First of all, I AM American—regardless of the color of my skin or the place of my birth. There is . . . nowhere else I would call home. . . . [Thus] I looked at the words, and I looked inwardly at myself, and I signed. . . . In the midst of great pain, there is also loss. The last question that the interviewer had for me was, "Do you want to change your name?" . . . I politely declined the name change, and we were done. That is the story of the naturalization of Saraswathy.[51]

It is also the story of thousands of other Indian Americans and of those immigrants who are becoming Indian Americans.

NOTES

Introduction: Across the Water

1. Quoted in Apte Poornima, "Panelist to South Asians: Develop a Voice That Shapes Public Opinion." *India New England News*, May 15, 2003. www.indianewengland.com/news/42 4048.html.

Chapter 1: From Mogul to Raj

2. Quoted in, South Asian History, edited and maintained by Shishir Thadani. http://india_resource.tripod.com/sahistory.html.
3. Quoted in South Asian History, "British Education in India."
4. Quoted in South Asian History, "The Colonial Legacy—Myths and Popular Beliefs."
5. Quoted in South Asian History, "The Colonial Legacy."

Chapter 2: The First Wave

6. Quoted in South Asian History, "The Colonial Legacy."
7. Quoted in Suzanne McMahon, "Echoes of Freedom: South Asian Pioneers in California, 1899–1965." www.lib.berkeley.edu/SSEAL/echoes/chapter2/chapter2.html.
8. Quoted in McMahon, "Echoes of Freedom."
9. Quoted in Parmatma Saran, *The Asian Indian Experience in the United States*. Cambridge, MA: Schenkman, 1985, p. 72.

10. Quoted in Saran, *The Asian Indian Experience*, p. 76.
11. Quoted in Joan M. Jensen, *Passage from India*. New Haven, CT: Yale University Press, 1988, p. 45.
12. Quoted in Pioneer Asian Indian Immigration to the Pacific Coast. www.lib.ucdavis.edu/punjab/pacific.html.

Chapter 3: Decades of Uncertainty

13. Quoted in Jaspal Singh, "History of the Ghadar Movement." www.punjab.org.uk/english/histGPty.html.
14. Quoted in McMahon, "Echoes of Freedom."

Chapter 4: The Second Wave Grows

15. Quoted in Saran, *The Asian Indian Experience*, p. 50.
16. Quoted in Saran, *The Asian Indian Experience*, p. 72.
17. Quoted in Sathi S. Dasgupta, *On the Trail of an Uncertain Dream: Indian Immigrant Experience in America*. New York: AMS Press, 1989, p. 45.
18. Quoted in Dasgupta, *On the Trail of an Uncertain Dream*, p. 54.
19. Quoted in Dasgupta, *On the Trail of an Uncertain Dream*, p. 55.
20. Padma Rangaswamy, *Namasté America: Indian Immigrants in an American Metropolis*. University Park: Pennsylvania State University Press, 2000, p. 94.

21. James Heitzman, *India: A Country Study.* Washington, DC: Library of Congress, 1994.
22. Quoted in Jean Bacon, *Life Lines: Community, Family, and Assimilation Among Asian Indian Immigrants.* New York: Oxford University Press, 1996, pp. 93–94.
23. Quoted in Dasgupta, *On the Trail of an Uncertain Dream*, pp. 172–73.

Chapter 5: Evolving Indian Values

24. Quoted in Saran, *The Asian Indian Experience*, p. 57.
25. The Balch Institute for Ethnic Studies, "Live Like the Banyan Tree." www.balchinstitute.org/museum/banyan/banyan_tree.html.
26. Quoted in Dasgupta, *On the Trail of an Uncertain Dream*, p. 85.
27. Quoted in Rangaswamy, *Namasté America*, p. 155.
28. Dasgupta, *On the Trail of an Uncertain Dream*, p. 134.
29. Quoted in Rangaswamy, *Namasté America*, p. 164.

Chapter 6: Between Two Worlds

30. Quoted in Bacon, *Life Lines*, p. 110.
31. Quoted in Saran, *The Asian Indian Experience*, p. 51.
32. Quoted in Rangaswamy, *Namasté America*, p. 170.
33. Quoted in Dasgupta, *On the Trail of an Uncertain Dream*, p. 125.
34. Quoted in Bacon, *Life Lines*, p. 158.
35. Quoted in Rangaswamy, *Namasté America*, p. 175.
36. Quoted in Rangaswamy, *Namasté America*, p. 176.
37. Quoted in Indian American Center for Political Awareness. www.iacfpa.org.
38. Quoted in Rangaswamy, *Namasté America*, p. 177.
39. Quoted in Bacon, *Life Lines*, pp. 218–19.
40. Quoted in Bacon, *Life Lines*, p. 102.
41. Quoted in Bacon, *Life Lines*, p. 66.
42. Quoted in Bacon, *Life Lines*, p. 67.
43. Quoted in Bacon, *Life Lines*, p. 68.
44. Quoted in Rangaswamy, *Namasté America*, p. 294.

Chapter 7: Into the American Mainstream

45. Bacon, *Life Lines*, p. 23.
46. Quoted in Congressional Caucus on India and Indian-Americans. www.usindiafriendship.net/congress/caucus/caucus.html.
47. Congressional Caucus on India and Indian-Americans.
48. Quoted in A.P. Kamath, "Women Writers of Indian Diaspora Create a Big Impact," Rediff on the Net, August 23, 1999. www.rediff.com
49. Quoted in Rangaswamy, *Namasté America*, p. 188.
50. Quoted in Rangaswamy, *Namasté America*, p. 189.
51. Saraswathy Ramanathan, "The Naturalization of Saraswathy," IADO Newsletter, Winter 1999, p. 6.

FOR FURTHER READING

Books

A.L. Basham, ed., *Cultural History of India.* Oxford: Oxford University Press, 1999. An overview of Indian culture, emphasizing religion, philosophy, social behavior, literature, art, music, politics, and science. Includes a section on the influence of Indian culture on the world.

William Goodwin, *India.* San Diego, CA: Lucent Books, 2000. Provides a complete history of India, from British colonization to the modern era, and an overview of the nation's geography, religion, ethnic diversity, and arts.

Susan Gordon, *Asian Indians.* New York: Franklin Watts, 1990. Offers comprehensive information on Indian immigrants, their culture, and experiences in the United States.

Mira Kamdar, *Motiba's Tattoos: A Granddaughter's Journey into Her Indian Family's Past.* New York: Public Affairs, 2000. The author's account of her family's immigration to the United States and their efforts to redefine their identities as Indian or American. Includes a positive look at the changing ideas of Indian American youth.

R. Viswanath, *Teenage Refugees and Immigrants from India Speak Out (In Their Own Voices).* New York: Rosen, 1997. A collection of interviews and personal accounts from Indian American teenagers who discuss why their families immigrated to the United States and how they have coped with life in their chosen country.

WORKS CONSULTED

Books

Meena Alexander, *The Shock of Arrival*. Boston: South End Press, 1996. A collection of stories and poems that sheds light on the Indian immigrant experience in the United States.

Jean Bacon, *Life Lines: Community, Family, and Assimilation Among Asian Indian Immigrants*. New York: Oxford University Press, 1996. A thorough exploration of issues important to the Indian immigrant, based on extensive interviews, included in the text, with six immigrant families.

Sathi S. Dasgupta, *On the Trail of an Uncertain Dream: Indian Immigrant Experience in America*. New York: AMS Press, 1989. A comprehensive study of the process of assimilation for Indian immigrants in America, emphasizing gender roles, parent-child relations, employment, and the reasons why they immigrated. Each section includes extensive personal quotes from people in the study.

James Heitzman, *India: A Country Study*. Washington. DC: Library of Congress, 1994.

Joan M. Jensen, *Passage from India*. New Haven, CT: Yale University Press, 1988. A comprehensive, readable history of pre-1965 Indian immigration, including U.S. immigration laws of the time, the social climate, and how the immigrants coped with legal and racial obstacles.

Sunaina Marr Maira, *Desis in the House: Indian American Youth Culture in New York City*. Philadelphia: Temple University Press, 2002. A detailed study of Indian American youth that explores issues of race, gender, and identity.

Padma Rangaswamy, *Namasté America: Indian Immigrants in an American Metropolis*. University Park: Pennsylvania State University Press, 2000. Discusses the Indian worldview versus the American mainstream and how differences between them affect the immigrant experience. Includes quotes from women, youth, and the elderly on issues such as work, family, society, India, dating, and marriage.

Parmatma Saran, *The Asian Indian Experience in the United States*. Cambridge, MA: Schenkman, 1985. A useful reference that profiles the history of immigration in the United States and gives an overview of Indian American demographics, residence in India, education, employment, family patterns, and leisure. Ten case studies that reflect these issues are included.

Periodicals

Daily Astorian, "'Hindu Alley' Men Were Peaceable (1906–1922)," April 26, 1973.

Jeff Giles, "Out of This World," *Newsweek*, August 5, 2002.

New York Times, "Emigrant Lifts Horizons of Village Girls," January 23, 2000.

Saraswathy Ramanathan, "The Naturalization of Saraswathy," IADO Newsletter, Winter 1999.

Mervyn Rothstein, "India's Post-Rushdie Generation: Young Writers Leave Magic Realism and Look at Reality," *New York Times*, July 3, 2000.

Anthony Spaeth, "Golden Diaspora," *Time*, March 7, 2001.

Internet Sources

The Balch Institute for Ethnic Studies, "Common Misconceptions about Indian Americans." www.balchinstitute.org/museum/banyan/banyanmisconceptions.html.

——— "Live Like the Banyan Tree." www.balchinstitute.org/museum/banyan/banyan_tree.html.

Indian Express, "Indian Toehold in U.S. Political Whirlpool," November 19, 2002. www.usinpac.com/11192002ie.asp.

A.P. Kamath, "Women Writers of Indian Diaspora Create a Big Impact," Rediff on the Net, August 23, 1999. www.rediff.com/

Suzanne McMahon "Echoes of Freedom: South Asian Pioneers in California, 1899–1965." www.lib.berkeley.edu/SSEAL/echoes/echoes/html.

Varun Nikore, Indian American Leadership Incubator. www.ialipac.org/IALITrainingConferenceAgenda.pdf.

Neil Parekh, "Community Must Ask More of Caucus," *News India-Times*, February 25, 2000. www.usindiafriendship.net/congress/caucus/parekhcaucus.html.

Pioneer Asian Indian Immigration to the Pacific Coast. www.lib.ucdavis.edu/punjab/pacific.html.

Apte Poornima, "Panelist to South Asians: Develop a Voice That Shapes Public Opinion." *India New England News*, May 15, 2003. www.indianewengland.com/news/424048.html.

Jaspal Singh, "History of the Ghadar Movement." www.punjab.org.uk/english/histGPty.html.

South Asian History, edited and maintained by Shishir Thadani. http://india_resource.tripod.com/sahistory.html.

Websites

Congressional Caucus on India and Indian-Americans (www.usindiafriendship.net/congress/caucus/caucus.html). Provides congressional news and links to Indian political organizations.

India Currents (www.indiacurrents.com). Dedicated to the concerns and interests of Indian Americans. Includes articles on spiritual, cultural, and national issues, the arts and youth.

Indian American Center for Political Awareness (www.iacfa.org.). National organization that encourages political awareness and participation of the Indian American community.

Indian Embassy (www.indianembassy.org). Provides articles and information on events and issues in both India and the United States, with an emphasis on foreign relations, terrorism, and immigration policy.

Indify (www.indify.org). A website devoted to improving the lives of Indian Americans by developing their leadership and community skills.

Indo-American Democratic Organization, Inc. (www.iado.org). Offers guidance and support for Indian American political activism. Promotes lobbying for immigration, education, and India-U.S. relations.

Jiva Ayurveda (www.ayurvedic.org). Furnishes advice and information pertaining to the practice of Indian medicine. Offers a newsletter, columns and articles, events listings, and an online pharmacy.

U.S.-India Friendship (www.usindiafriendship.net). A resource on Indo-American relations, with news about congressional acts, media portrayals, viewpoints, and an online discussion forum.

INDEX

organizations and, 91–92

preservation of, 66, 69, 73, 94–95

Daily Astorian (newspaper), 33–34

dance, 62–63, 77

Dandekar, Swati, 84

Dasgupta, Sathi, 64, 66

desi (second-generation Indian
Americans), 70–82

*Desis in the House: Indian American
Youth Culture in New York City*
(Maira), 77

Dham, Vinod, 91

dharma, 39

Digby, William, 27

Dossani, Rafiq, 57

educational level, 55–56

Ellis Island, 31

English language, 10, 55–56

filmmaking, 88–90

Gandhi, Indira, 48

Gandhi, Mohandas K., 40–41

Ganguly, Ranjit, 86

gender role differences, 64–65

generation gap, 70–82

Ghadar (newspaper), 41–42

Ghadar Movement, 41–42, 44, 47

Gilman, Benjamin, 93

God of Small Things, The (Roy), 89

Gurdwaras, 60–61

hate crimes, 86–87
  see also racism

Heitzman, James, 56–57

Hindi, 20, 60

Hinduism
  beliefs of, 68
  dance and, 62
  early immigrants and, 47
  history of, 13, 69
  persecution of followers of, 15–16
  preservation of heritage of, 91–92
  Tamil and, 47

Home Rule League, 44

Hussain, Zakir, 91

identification, as Americans, 94–95

immigrant children. *See* second
  generation

immigrant groups
  business associations of, 61–62

languages of, 20

problems of, after independence, 48, 49–50

products and technology of, 14, 16

religion of, 12–13, 15, 47

starvation and disease in, 26–27, 28, 29

Suez Canal impact upon, 22–23

India: A Country Study (Heitzman), 56–57

India Association, 44, 91

Indian American Center for Political Awareness, 61

Indian American Forum, 59

Indian American Forum for Political Education, 85

Indian American Leadership Incubator, 85

Indian American mainstream socialization support groups, 92–94

Indian American Political Forum for Political Action, 61

Indian Americans

challenges of, 11

first immigrants, 29–37

statistics about, 8–9, 10

success of, as immigrant group, 8–11

see also immigrants after 1965; immigrants of earlier eras

Indian independence movement, 44–45

Indian National Congress, 47

Indian Spiritual Organization, 92

Indify (Indian American support group), 92–94

Indo-American Center, 94

Indo-American Democratic Organization (IADO), 86

Indus Entrepreneurs, 88

intergenerational disagreements, 70–82

Interpreter of Maladies (Lahiri), 89

Islam, 13, 15, 47

isolation (vs. cultural preservation), 66

journalism, 89

kathak, 62–63

Khan, Ali Akbar, 91

Khan, Mubarak Ali, 44

Khan, Ustad Irshad, 91

Komagata Maru (ship), 43

Lahiri, Jhumpa, 89

(1923), 42–44

U.S. Immigration and Nationality Act
   of 1952, 46

Vivekananda, Swami, 34

women's roles, 63–65

work ethics, 58

writers, 88–89

"yellow peril," 34

youth culture, 70–82

Zakaria, Fareed, 89

PICTURE CREDITS

About the Authors

Scott Ingram has written for young people for more than twenty-five years. He lives in Portland, Connecticut.

Christina M. Girod received her undergraduate degree from the University of California at Santa Barbara. She worked with speech- and language-impaired students and taught elementary school for six years in Denver, Colorado. She has written feature articles, short biographies, and organizational and country profiles for educational multimedia materials. The topics she has covered include politicians, humanitarians, environmentalists, entertainers, and geography. She has also written several titles for Lucent Books, on subjects such as Native Americans, entertainers, careers, and disabilities. She also wrote *Connecticut, South Carolina,* and *Georgia,* part of the Thirteen Colonies series. Girod lives in Santa Maria, California, with her husband, Jon Pierre, and daughter, Joni.